No Time to Kill

No Time to Kill

By John and Emery Bonett

WALKER AND COMPANY,
New York

First published in the United States of America in 1972 by the
Walker Publishing Company, Inc.

ISBN: 0-8027-5251-9

Library of Congress Catalog Card Number: 70-186191

Printed in the United States of America.

Contents

Chief Characters in the Story

Eldred Poole	A consequential little man
Clarice Poole	His inconsequential wife
James Rowley	A successful writer
Gregory Warrack	A writer achieving success
Basil Seaton	A solicitor
Colin Dennison	A young sociologist; Clarice's nephew
Thersie Sallis	A girl on her own
Thomasina Clegg	A schoolmistress
Bill Eddow	Courier for 'Phoebus Abroad'
Juan Carosco	A contented man
Carmen Carosco	His happy wife
Millie Best	A girl with a slight problem
Antonia Murray	A friend of Basil
Perce Strongitharm	Brother craftsmen
Jack Strongitharm	
Escipión	Manager of the Hotel Adrián
Salvador Borges	Inspector in the Brigade of Criminal Investigation
Shadow	His dog

1

Sunday morning, 10th September

"**D**ID YOU hear what I said, dear?" demanded the short, consequential man who was holding the wheel of the car with gloved hands.

"Yes, Eldred."

"And you agree?"

"Yes, dear." Clarice Poole answered the question which had been put to her interminably since they left Calais the day before yesterday. She had her reservations about the matter, but had no intention of mentioning them while her husband was driving.

As they drove on she tried to consider her husband dispassionately, knowing that objectivity about a man to whom one had been married for so long was impossible. He was mean about money matters, but never where she herself was concerned. He was something of a snob without having either the background or the intellect which might have provided a reason if not an excuse. His attitude to a number of everyday things was indefensible, but perhaps mainly due to his upbringing. She had met his father only briefly before the latter's death and had disliked and despised him. Then there was Eldred's behaviour with other women. He liked to be thought a Don Juan, though, as she very well knew, he was a man without much masculinity. But he had one great virtue for which she would never cease to be thankful: his sulks never lasted for more than half an hour. And that, she told

1

herself, is something that many of the wives I know can't say about their husbands. In any case, what has he got in me? I'm feather-brained, untidy, unpunctual. I can't cook. I've been unable to give him a child. If we'd had a family, if we hadn't both had too much money, we'd have had less time to think, less time to kill.

"You're very quiet," said Eldred. "Thinking about something?"

"Only about time, dear."

"You don't have to worry your little head about that. I'm well up to the schedule I made out before we started." He glanced at the clock on the dashboard. "Twenty minutes ahead, in fact. We should be at the frontier in half an hour. If there's not one of those long queues there, we'll be at Cala Felix by lunch-time." He edged the car to the left as they caught up with a crawling lorry. "Tell me—is it safe to pass?"

"Yes, dear." Clarice, who had been listening without taking in what was said, answered automatically.

Eldred swung the wheel and accelerated. The express coach travelling in the opposite direction swept past a foot away from their mudguard.

"My god, Clarice!" He drew in his breath sharply. "You nearly had us killed. What on earth were you thinking about?"

"I'm sorry, dear. I didn't see it," she apologized in a small voice.

"You'd better have your eyes tested when we get back to England," he told her.

"Yes, dear," she agreed meekly.

It was not until they had passed the frontier that Eldred spoke again. "What time did Colin say he'd turn up tomorrow?" he asked.

"He said he'd send a card to let us know."

Eldred nodded. "Well, he can't expect us to stay in all day waiting for him. I want to pass this van, Clarice. Will you look very carefully to see if there is anything coming. We want to stay alive."

Cala Felix lies not so many miles north of Palamós. The small, sheltered bay faces southeast. On the right, as one looks at the sea, rises Cap Rubí, an eighty foot high promontory of grey rock streaked with seams of red and yellow sandstone.

Not many foreigners reach Cala Felix, though a number catch sight of it from the tourist launches which ply between the larger coastal resorts. On the landward side the dirt road that runs off the north-south highway to the centre of the bay offers little attraction to the motorist. Not only does it appear to come to an end at a heap of ruins after some hundred yards, but it is pitted with possibly the largest number of potholes, and the deepest, of any track in that region of rough and unready roads.

If one were to ask why the potholes are not filled in, the answers would be that the local authorities see no reason to adopt the road, and that Juan Carosco who owns the land up to the high-tide mark prefers to keep it that way. He is satisfied with the place as it is and has no wish to develop his property further.

It was some years ago that to his surprise he found himself, as a result of two fatal accidents, the owner of Cala Felix. At that time he was an insurance agent with a handful of pesetas in his pocket and a host of acquaintances, one of whom also had a host of acquaintances and a suggestion. Juan considered the latter and reached a decision. He sold a piece of land at the south-west end of the bay to a company who wished to build an hotel. With the money from the sale he built in successive steps, on the other side of the bay, six pleasant bungalows fronting onto a narrow, sandy road that ended in a banjo where a car could turn. These he sold to foreigners, three of them English. Then, with sufficient cash in hand, he put up, between the hotel and the dirt road, six more bungalows for letting to summer visitors. When this proved a successful venture, he built for himself and his young English wife a house in the centre of the bay, to which the following year he added the Bar Felix. A shop followed, with a flat above it, in which, out of affection, he installed his sister Pura and her idle husband Luis. Now, with the interest on a substantial capital sum, the rentals from the summer lettings, a small profit from the bar and a minimal one from the shop, he was able to view the rushing world from a comfortable distance.

On this sunny morning in September he was standing on the beach watching his seven-year-old daughter and her younger brother as they paddled a rubber boat in circles some fifteen yards away. The outboard motor from his white dinghy lay on a plastic sheet by his feet, overhauled and ready to be replaced should someone wish to hire the boat. To his left, beside a red buoy, bobbed the motor launch in which he occasionally took small parties up or down the coast and which he was prepared to hire to visitors of whose seamanship he had assured himself. Within a week or so it would be taken out of the water. For the season was now almost over. Incessant rain during the past month had driven the sun-seekers further south. Fine weather had returned four days ago, but too late to bring holiday bookings for the tail end of the summer. Next Sunday the last of the package-tour parties, the backbone of its business, would be leaving the Hotel Adrián, and only two of the renting bungalows would be occupied.

Juan looked along the beach. Bill Eddow, the courier in charge of the small 'Phoebus Abroad' party at the hotel, was strolling by the water's edge. The thin, pert Beryl and her even thinner boyfriend Cyril were making their way past the hotel to the narrow cleft in the rock that led from Cala Felix to the small cove known as La Caleta. Since the cove was stony except for a patch of sand little larger than a Badminton court, the extreme narrowness of the opening discouraged all but the slender from visiting it.

Calling to the children not to take the boat further from the beach, Juan turned and, going up the steps to the terrace, entered the bar. The barroom was spacious and its atmosphere friendly. Behind the walnut-topped counter bottled liquids of every hue and shining glasses gleamed a welcome doubled by a long backing mirror. Pausing in the doorway, Juan called to his wife.

"Back in a sec," Carmen sang out from the kitchen. "Will you come and give Enrique a hand in moving the fridge?"

She was rubbing at a small stain on the bar counter when a tall, good-looking man, deeply tanned, strode in. "I've run out of fags, Carmen. Got a packet of filter-tips?"

"Here you are, Greg—and I've got a parcel the *recadero* brought in. Looks like books."

Glancing at the label, he took out a penknife. "It is. Must be copies of the novel." He cut the string and tugged open the wrapping.

"Ooh, let's look." She almost snatched the topmost of the half-dozen copies. "Fancy having a book with your name on it. *No End of a World* by Gregory Warrack," she read aloud. "What's it about?" Without waiting for an answer, she went on, "They haven't half given you a rude cover. He hasn't a stitch on—and just look at all that blood! Can I read it, please?" Her pretty face was alight with irrestible pleading.

Gregory sighed and melted. This was his first novel, and a writer faced with his initial batch of author's copies wants to handle them before anyone else does, to read the blurb if he hasn't written it himself, and to indulge in a little private gloating. But he also needs the praise of a sympathetic and not over-critical reader. "All right," he said. "But promise to let me have it back as soon as you've read it and not to lend it to anyone else."

"It's a promise, Greg. Cross my heart. And I'll let you know what I think of it."

He grinned. "If you don't like it, don't tell me. If you do, tell me several times." He picked up the remaining books. "See you later." Waving to the children, he strolled back to the hotel and went to his room.

At two o'clock he clipped together some typewritten sheets and snapped the lid over the typewriter. The chef's elder daughter who worked in Palafrugell and motor-cycled out for a free lunch in the hotel kitchen brought out the post and any newspapers ordered by the visitors. She should have arrived by now.

Going along to the reception desk he found it untenanted and, reaching across, picked Saturday's *Daily Record* out of a pigeon-hole. Through the glazed double doors of the dining-room he could see the 'Phoebus Abroad' party at the centre table. At the far end Bill Eddow thoughtfully rotated his wine-glass. On either side of him the two stout ladies whose names Gregory had not troubled to find out were champing their way through piled plates of *paella,* the regular second course on Sunday at every Spanish hotel he had ever visited. Next to them their thick-set husbands were similarly and silently engaged. Beryl and Cyril sat with their backs to the doorway. On the opposite side of the table Miss Clegg's intelligent face was lit with slightly shocked amusement at some remark of Beryl's. Next to Miss Clegg the pretty blonde, Millie, put down her fork and, looking up, flashed a delighted smile at Gregory.

Returning to his room, he changed into bathing shorts and, going onto the balcony, settled down to read the paper over a lunch of an apple and some biscuits. Disliking a large meal in the middle of the day, he had arranged *demi-pension* with the manager, Escipión. He had also taken a room at the extreme right-hand end of the hotel as one faced the sea. Here he could work at his typewriter without disturbing the other guests whose rooms were all at the opposite end of the building.

Finishing his lunch, he screwed the small debris into a scrap of paper. In due course he would take his long daily swim. Meantime there were a number of tangles in the present story to be unknotted. On film scripts he had always worked with another writer or as part of a team whose members sparked ideas off or out of one another, and he missed the stimulus of collaboration. It was, however, some time since he had been offered a scripting job. But, if his first novel were the success that his agents and publishers predicted, he hoped once more to find himself in demand. Well, he must get down to work. But why not swim first and let exercise clear his mind?

Passing the signpost that pointed to Monells, Basil Seaton took his right hand from the steeringwheel and wiped it on his trousered thigh. It was hot, damned hot. He decided to stop for a glass of beer at La Bisbal. An ugly town, he said to himself. No, that wasn't entirely true. So many Spanish towns and villages looked ugly in bright sunshine when one could see only too plainly the peeling plaster and paint. But in moonlight or when the sun was low, the *pueblos* had an air of romantic beauty. Perhaps that was why the Spaniards kept what to northerners seemed such astonishingly late hours. He jammed his foot on the brake as a horse and cart turned from the right onto the road some yards ahead. A moment later as he hooted and passed the cart the driver glanced down expressionlessly. His was the face of Spain, the face that carries from birth the message, 'This Spaniard is authorized to do just whatever he pleases.' It was one of the reasons why Basil liked Spain. Independence and personal pride were dying qualities in other countries of Western Europe. Slowing down as a child darted across the road, he parked outside the vast arcaded building that is one of the unavoidable sights of La Bisbal.

Sitting at a shaded café table, he was half-way through a bottle of beer when a hand clapped his shoulder. The thin, hollow-faced man who stood smiling down pulled out a chair with a tired sigh. "I saw your car, Basil, and hoped to find you not far away. You passed me some miles back and I blew and blew the horn, but you were clearly practising for Le Mans."

"James." Basil's pleasure was manifest. He signalled to the waiter to bring another beer. "I thought you were going to take it slowly across France." Looking at the wasted face and concealing his concern, he asked lightly, "When did you leave London?"

"Thursday morning. I rang your office before you left, but they said you wouldn't be in until later. Yes, I did travel faster than I'd planned, but I got sick of my own company.

I'll take it easy when we get to Cala Felix."

"You look a great deal better than when I saw you last week," said Basil untruthfully. "A few quiet days in the sun and you should be yourself again. When Carmen wrote the other day she said there'd be very few people in the bungalows and only a small party at the hotel."

"Yes, I know one—" James cleared his throat. "I know one should be sorry for Juan and Carmen if business is slack. But quiet is what I need—and I'll have your company. And you said Antonia was joining you soon, didn't you?"

"Tomorrow. And the Pooles will be returning today. Eldred rang me a few days ago to say so."

"Oh, Eldred." James's tone was not enthusiastic. "If only he wouldn't talk so much about the Stock Exchange. I suppose he's a pretty harmless little man—in spite of his dreadful habit of referring to Clarice as 'my lady wife'—but he does waste one's time. And I haven't got time to waste. I've got a book just about finished, and I want to do the final touching up while I'm away."

"I don't know how you find time to write books and do as much film work as you do."

James grinned. "I'm just naturally garrulous on paper. When you're working in the studios there are hours, sometimes days, when nobody wants to see you around. But you've got to be there in case someone decides to turn the story inside out. So you're left on your own to go whoring, or play solitaire, or prop up the nearest bar—or to get down to some other work, which is what I do. I turn out books as a kind of insurance. People will always go on reading—especially lonely folk." He drained his glass. "Shall we move on? I'll follow, and you can tell Carmen I'll be along later."

"Right you are." Basil rose. For the rest of the journey he was going to drive sedately, keeping an eye on the driving mirror and not losing sight of James. They had known one another for more than twenty years. They had been on holiday together when they found Cala Felix and decided to buy their bungalows.

That had been the year after the death of James's wife,

with whom Basil had been vainly in love.

Feet tucked beneath her, Carmen sat on the cushioned settee in the bar, reading *No End of a World*. Hearing footsteps on the terrace, she closed the book and laid it face down on the counter. She turned to find herself in a close embrace. A hand under her buttocks pulled her forward and a wet mouth covered hers. Intolerable seconds passed before she was freed.

"You're looking more wonderful than ever." Eldred stood back to admire. A tongue passed across the plump lips as he slipped a small packet into her hand with a whispered "A little fragrance for my rose."

"Thank you, Eldred." It had been in Carmen's mind to say something more. Only the sudden slap of a foot on the floor and the subsequent sight of Juan glowering in the doorway to the kitchen made her hold her tongue.

Eldred followed her glance. "Oh, hello, Juan," he smiled. "How are you?"

Juan gave the briefest of nods, then turned back into the kitchen.

"Not quite himself today?" enquired Eldred, stroking his clipped silver moustache.

"He's got something on his mind," Carmen answered shortly. "Can I get you a drink? And what about one for Clarice? She'll be along, won't she?"

"I'm here, and I'd like a sherry, please." Clarice kissed Carmen warmly. "Now tell us all the gossip. Who's here?"

"No one you know just now. There's a small party of tourists at the hotel." She moved to the other side of the counter, asked Eldred what he was having and poured out. "Basil should be along at any moment, and James is coming. Oh, you knew that, did you? That's all of you lot." She did not have to explain that by 'you lot' she meant the English buyers of the original bungalows. "Then there's the lettings. Some people called Sallis are coming for the best part of three weeks. They've been here before, but not at the same time as you. And," she chuckled, "there's Perce and

Jack. They're a couple of cards. I bet when you meet them Perce will say, 'The name's Strongitharm,' and Jack will grunt, 'Ay, strong i' the arm, but a mite weak in the head.' They're out diving most of the day, but they'll be in before supper."

"And that's all, is it?" Clarice sounded disappointed.

"No, there's Greg—Gregory Warrack. He's a writer, staying at the hotel. He works all mornings—afternoons too, half the time. Fancies himself, but he's all right."

"We were hoping there'd be a few young people here," said Clarice. "My nephew Colin's coming to stay with us for a week. He's been walking across France. The postcard you put in our bungalow said he hoped to arrive tomorrow."

"He'll be O.K. There's one in the tour party that won't let him get lonely—and that's Millie. You wait till he sees her— then you won't be seeing much of him day or night."

"She doesn't sound very *nice*," Clarice said dubiously.

"She'll be nice to Colin." Carmen grinned. "There's nothing wrong there that he can't put right if he likes a bit of fun."

"Of course he does." Eldred touched his moustache with a loving hand. "Just like his old uncle," he caught Clarice's eye, "before I married." He cocked his head and stepped towards the window. "There's a car coming. No, two cars. By Jove, it's Basil *and* James. I must go and welcome them."

"*We* must go," Clarice said gently. "But we mustn't keep them talking. They'll be hot and tired, and they'll want to wash and change."

It was half an hour later when Basil came into the bar. Carmen, closing her book, greeted him warmly. For a moment she scarcely recognized the man who followed. He was sallow and emaciated, but the grin on his face was familiar and cheering. "Oh, James," she exclaimed when she had kissed him, "you've had a bad time."

"They thought I was a goner," he said gaily, "but I fooled them. In a month's time I'll be my usual handsome, magnetic self. All I need now is a whisky and soda, and Basil will have a gin."

"And make 'em both large." Basil pulled out a stool for James and, taking out a handkerchief, mopped the top of his head. "D'you think you could manage a couple of omelettes, Carmen?"

"Give me five minutes." She trotted into the kitchen. They were her favourite visitors—and James looked dreadfully ill. She was going to look after him.

When Basil, with a murmured "Back in a minute," went over to the cloakroom, James picked up the book that Carmen had left on the counter. After a glance at the dustjacket he began to read the blurb. When she returned with knives, forks and napkins, he asked if it were her book.

"No, it's Greg's. It's just come out, and he lent it me."

He gazed at her with raised eyebrows. "Do you mean that Gregory Warrack's here?"

"He's at the hotel—been there for three weeks."

"Well, I'm damned." James paused, then smiled. "He's an old acquaintance of mine. We've worked together in pictures. I'd like to read the book if I may."

Carmen hesitated. "I promised not to lend it."

"Look," James said easily. "If Gregory were here he'd lend it to me like a shot. I'm a fast reader and I promise you'll have it back before this evening. O.K.?"

"O.K. then. If I see him before you do shall I tell him you're here? He'll be in before dinner. About seven's his usual time."

"I'll be here before then—with the book." James slipped it into his pocket as Basil returned and Enrique came in from the kitchen with two large golden-brown omelettes.

Twenty minutes later they were about to leave when Carmen gave an exclamation. "I nearly forgot your telegram, Basil. Came for you yesterday." She took it from between two bottles on the shelf.

He tore it open. Momentarily his jaw tightened, then he gave a shrug. "Nothing urgent," he said casually.

Leaving the shop where Luis had risen unwillingly from

his chair to sell him a packet of cigarettes, Bill Eddow stood indecisively. He was spending too much money. The last party of tourists whom he had shepherded at Llafranch had been mean with their parting tips, and he had a feeling that the present small party would be equally parsimonious. He shrugged. After all, he wasn't doing much to enliven their holiday. None of them wished to play organized games, or to be taken to the shops with which he had commission arrangements. None of them wanted to visit a night club—except Millie. And he had to be very careful about Millie if he hoped to be employed again by "Phoebus Abroad'.

Jobs for a man of forty-six were not easily found, especially if all one could offer were two foreign languages and a variety of experiences about which it was better to maintain silence. The romp in July with the little widow from Streatham, if rather more expensive than he had intended, had been enormously enjoyable. Unfortunately, some busybody member of the party had complained that Bill devoted more time to his own pleasures than to his duties, and he had received a letter from the Tours Manager reminding him curtly of the terms of his employment. For that reason he was behaving circumspectly, taking care not to be alone with Millie or, if he were unable to avoid her direct approaches, to ensure that they were of such brief duration that nothing could have occurred which would bring a blush to the cheek, or a pen to the hand, of any self-appointed guardian of others' morals.

He turned his head at the sound of an approaching car. It stopped beside him, and a smiling, frog-like face leaned from the driver's seat. "*Señor* Eddow?"

"Yes, I'm Bill Eddow."

"I recognized you from the description of a mutual friend." The smile was on the lips, but not in the eyes that were taking in Bill's snub-nosed face, the thinning hair and the look of weather-worn amiability. "He suggested that you might be able to undertake a small commission for me—for a suitable fee, of course. If you have time, perhaps we could have a drink together."

A few minutes later Bill, seated on the hotel terrace, glass in hand, was listening, then smiling. "But why do you ask me to do this?" he enquired.

"I would do it myself, but I have to be in Madrid on business. Our friend told me that you can handle a launch, and that there is one here you can hire. I will pay the hire-charge." He put a thousand-peseta note on the table. "Our friend also told me that you were a sportsman—but, if you feel that the suggestion isn't sporting enough—" His hand hovered over the note.

"I'll do it." Bill pocketed the note. Juan, he was thinking, will lend me the launch for the cost of the fuel.

"I would not like you to fail."

"If your other arrangements don't fail, I shan't. It'll be a piece of cake."

"A piece of cake." The other man laughed as he rose. "That is an expression I did not know." He led the way to the car. "Goodbye, *Señor* Eddow."

"Goodbye." Bill bent down to the window. "I don't think you mentioned your name."

"García."

"And the name of our mutual friend?"

"Also García." The frog-face beamed, and the car shot off.

Bill watched it disappear. García. In Spain the name was as common as that of Smith in England. For a fleeting moment he felt doubt. No, there was nothing ticklish in what he had been asked to do. There was nothing to it—except a useful little bit of cash.

2

Sunday afternoon and evening, 10ᵗʰ September

"**W**HAT TIME does the trip start tomorrow, Mr Eddow?" Miss Clegg called down the luncheon table.

"Nine o'clock." Bill looked round the party. "You're all going, aren't you?"

"Not going to cost us anything?" The stouter of the two thick-set men asked through a mouthful of spaghetti.

"It's all included in your booking, Mr Smurthwaite. The hotel will provide packed lunches, and there's a café where you can get any kind of drink."

"What's there to see?" asked the less stout man. "Just a bunch of ruins?"

"There's a fine beach, and—"

"It's one of the most fascinating places in this part of Spain," Miss Clegg interrupted enthusiastically. "When Cato landed there in the second century it had been inhabited for several hundred years. Then the Romans colonized it. There's an interesting museum and some quite good mosaic work—though they don't look after it properly. I've been there twice before and know something of its history."

"Then you've taken a load off my mind," Bill said smoothly. "You can tell them much more about it than I could. I'm terribly afraid I shan't be able to come with you tomorrow. Got to see to some business down the coast. Sorry to miss the trip, but you couldn't be in better hands

14

than Miss Clegg's."

"Thank you, Mr Eddow." There was a cynical glint in Miss Clegg's eye. She knew from Carmen that Bill had a girlfriend in a neighbouring resort. She was also certain that the rest of the party would quickly tire of viewing the remains of the past and would elect to spend most of the day on the beach. Neither the Smurthwaites nor their friends the Arkells were built for walking or mentally equipped to distinguish, or wish to distinguish, Greek from Roman. Beryl was going only because Cyril wished to see Ampurias. Millie would come rather than be left alone. Poor Millie, so ripe for the plucking, so ready to be plucked; she could never have anticipated a holiday party of which the sole unharnessed male would prefer Beryl's company to hers. She was what the Restoration poets would have called 'a salt wench'.

A dust-caked white Renault drew up before the Bar Felix. A girl slid from the driving-seat, stretched herself vigorously and, passing combing fingers through her glossy, dark-brown hair, breathed deeply. She was tall and slim. Her tanned face emphasized the whiteness of her even teeth. Her cheekbones were set too widely apart for conventional standards of beauty, her mouth was too generous, the bridge of her nose too strong. But she exuded such vitality, such obvious enjoyment in being alive, that no eye could rest on her and fail to remain for some pleasurable moments.

Carmen looked up from her son's pair of shorts which she was darning on the terrace. "Thersie Sallis," she cried, running to kiss her. "You're a sight for sore eyes. Come and sit down, and I'll get you something cold to drink, and we can have a good old natter."

"I'd better let Mummy and Daddy know I'm here—then I'll be back." Thersie gazed round the familiar scene. Nothing had changed.

"They're not here. Didn't you know? I had a letter from your Mum yesterday, and she said she'd written to you."

"I left Madrid two days ago to visit some friends." Thersie remained standing. "There's nothing wrong, is there?"

15

she asked anxiously.

"Nothing," Carmen assured her. "Your Dad was asked to give a lecture and, as it was some sort of honour, he didn't want to say no. But they'll be here by next weekend, and you can have your meals with us until they come. Sleep here, too, if you like."

"Thanks a lot," Thersie said gratefully. "But I think I'll stay in the bungalow. Now tell me about yourself and the children and who's here and what they're like."

An hour passed while they gossiped, and then Thersie drove the short distance to the bungalow her parents had rented. She finished unloading the car and was closing the boot when a shadow came between her and the sun. She glanced up to see a sun-browned, smiling face. The man's hair was damp: he carried mask and flippers, and a towel was slung over one shoulder.

"Hallo. Just arrived?" he enquired. "Can I give you a hand with your luggage?"

"No, thanks. It's all in." She inspected him frankly. This must be the writer of whom Carmen had spoken. A handsome man, she reflected—and he knows it.

"My name's Gregory Warrack," he told her. "I'm staying at the hotel. Are you here on your own?"

"For a moment. My parents will be here later."

"Well, see you around." He hitched the towel further up his shoulder. "If there's anything I can do for you, let me know." He smiled and went off.

It occurred to Thersie as she went indoors that he would have found little difficulty in prolonging the conversation if he had known that she would be alone in the bungalow for the next few nights.

"Where are you, Clarice?" Eldred called fussily from the sitting-room after dinner.

"Just finishing off the unpacking. Shan't be a moment." She hung up his ties on the patent tie rack without which he never travelled, glanced at herself in the mirror and trotted into the sitting-room.

"You know I want us to make our wills tonight and have them witnessed," he said, putting down a pen with an expression of itching patience.

"Yes, I know, dear."

Eldred had expatiated monotonously on the subject during their drive through France. Like many self-absorbed people he had put off making a will year after year. Although he would never have acknowledged it, his reluctance was partly due to a superstitious feeling that the signing of one's final testament is an open invitation to Death. It was in part the kind of procrastination not uncommon among childless couples or those who have no kin with whom they are on terms of affection. There is also an unthinking assumption that, if one of a marriage partnership dies without making a will, the survivor will inherit the deceased's estate. It is not until somebody one knows dies intestate and a hitherto unconsidered relative turns up to receive his or her legal share of the estate that the facts are brought home. Such a case had come to Eldred's notice the evening before he and Clarice left for Spain. With all the bustle of a man who has done scarcely a stroke of work during his life Eldred tore headlong into action, rushed to a stationer's shop and bought a couple of ready-made will forms.

"I'm sure," he said at the beginning of the journey and repeated hourly throughout the day, "that the simplest thing by far is for each of us to leave everything to the other. Then whoever's left can carry out any wishes that the other has expressed." The theme had been so ceaselessly hammered home that Clarice had kept her thoughts to herself.

"I've written my will," he now said, holding it up as if it were a presentation certificate. " 'I give and bequeath all of which I die possessed to my wife Clarice Huntingdon Poole'. That's all it's necessary to say. Cut it short, and there'll be no legal arguments."

"Oughtn't it to be 'my widow'?" Clarice asked.

"You'll be my wife when I sign this, silly one. If you were my widow I'd be dead now."

"Oh, yes—I see."

"Then sit down like a good little girl and complete this form." He rose and, waiting until she took the chair, pointed to the words printed in Gothic lettering and began to dictate: " 'all of which I die possessed to my dear husband Eldred Kitchener Poole'. Now blot it. No, dear." He snatched the pen from her hand. "You don't write those words." Picking up the paper, he waved it to dry the ink and, folding both forms, placed them in his inside breast pocket. "We'll go along to the bar now and have our signatures witnessed. We must have English witnesses, of course."

When the Pooles reached the Bar Felix, Beryl and Cyril were at a table in the corner. Miss Clegg was talking to Carmen when Eldred interrupted them. They listened, concealing smiles, to his long-winded preamble and were at length permitted to add their names, occupations and addresses to the documents.

"What shall I put as my occupation?" Carmen asked mischievously. "Barmaid?"

Eldred was not amused. "In these particular circumstances I think 'house-wife' would be appropriate." Taking the completed papers, he returned them to his pocket and commanded drinks, finding himself unwillingly having to include in his order not only Basil and James who came in together but Thersie who arrived from the kitchen a few seconds later.

Shortly, James was able to slip into Carmen's hand the book he had borrowed.

"What d'you think of it?" she enquired.

"Not original," he replied dryly. "But a liberal hand with blood and sex. It should make quite a bit of money."

"Evenin' all." Two broad-shouldered men in twin cerise shirts advanced in step to the counter. "Couple of beers, ducks, and make it slippy," said one of them. "Our throats is like emery paper."

"This is Perce and Jack." Carmen introduced them to the newcomers.

Perce nodded round genially. "Strongitharm's the name—wi'out a 'postrophe."

"Ay," said Jack. "Strong i' the arm right enough, but a mite weak in the head."

Carmen winked at Clarice, then, turning to Jack, "Had a good day, love?"

"Fair enough. Took some likely pictures. Had a bit of trouble with the engine, but we got that sorted."

"That reminds me, Carmen." Eldred raised his voice over the chatter. "I'd like to hire the small boat tomorrow morning. Thought I'd take Clarice to see some friends who've built a house down the coast."

"I think that's O.K. if it's a fine day, but wait till we can check with Juan." Eldred had taken the boat out earlier in the season, but Carmen knew that Juan would not trust him with it unless the sea were as calm as a mill-pond and likely to remain so.

"Oh, it'll be fine," Eldred pronounced with the assurance of a man who in London never went without an umbrella. "Would you like to join us, James?" To take a well-known writer to his friends' house would put a feather in his social cap.

"Thank you very much—but no." James shook his head. "I intend to spend tomorrow doing absolutely nothing. A Lilo and a sun umbrella in undisturbed quiet in La Caleta, with a book that I probably shan't read." A sudden turning of heads made him look round.

Gregory, who had entered while James was speaking, came slowly towards him, an expression of bewilderment and uncertainty on his face. "James! It is James, isn't it?" He shook hands limply; then, making an obvious effort to regain composure, he went on, "Good god, man. I'm stunned and absolutely delighted. I thought you were—I mean I read your obituary in *Cine-Stage*."

"So did I." James chuckled. "And I've had a swelled head ever since. I damned nearly did snuff out. Caught some bug in South America and was bunged into hospital. They thought I'd kicked the bucket, and some bloody idiot told the Press so. Now I've got a clean bill of health, and I'm here for a month of fresh air and sea." He looked appraisingly at Gregory. "How are things going—and what are you doing here?"

"I'm at the hotel, taking a sort of busman's holiday, trying to get something down on paper." He made an expressive gesture. "The holiday's going better than the paperwork."

"We must have a talk about things later." James glanced round. "I expect you know everyone here except Basil." He introduced them, and conversation became general.

"Can I do any shopping for anyone tomorrow?" asked Thersie. "I'm going into San Feliu in the morning to look up a friend."

"Nothing for me, thanks," said Basil. "In any case I have a train to meet at Flassá."

"Heavens!" Clarice had picked up a newspaper. "Listen to this, Eldred." Her excited cry brought silence as she read out the headline 'Downchester Bank Robbery'. "It's *our* bank—and I was *there* and didn't know anything about it."

"It can't have happened while you were in the bank, my dear," Eldred said dogmatically, "or you would have noticed something even if you were in one of your day-dreams."

"I didn't say I was *in* the bank, dear. I went there for a cheque-book, but they hadn't opened although it was after half-past nine. There was another customer waiting, and he rapped on the window several times. And there were some ladders leaning up against the front, and buckets and things as if men were in the middle of cleaning that ugly black marble. The paper says they were the robbers." She nodded triumphantly. "They say the bank messenger who gets there early let two of them in to use the lavatory, and they put a cloth over his face and shut him in the stationery store in the basement and did the same to the rest of the staff as they arrived. Then they took the keys of the safe and the night safe and helped themselves."

"Did they get away with much?" asked Carmen.

"They say about ten thousand pounds in old notes. They didn't touch the new ones. Then they left by the side door in Market Street—it's a corner building and the main doors where I was waiting are in the High Street."

"Surely someone saw them when they were putting up the ladders," said Basil. "How many of them were there?"

"Three men and a boy, it says—and I must have seen one of them." Her voice rose. "There was a man leaving the side door as I got tired of waiting and went off to the shops. I told him there was a customer in front, and he said there'd been some trouble with the safe but they'd be open in a few minutes."

"What did this man look like?" Thersie asked.

"Like a workman. White overalls and a cap." Clarice thought for a moment. "He was peeling off a rubber glove. I caught a glimpse of a ring on his little finger and—oh, yes, he had those metal-framed glasses they give you on the National Health."

"You were pretty observant," Gregory remarked. "Would you recognize him if you saw him again?"

"I think I *might.*"

"Don't you think you ought to let the police know what you saw?" Basil asked quietly as he replaced a handkerchief in the pocket of his shirt.

"The police?" Clarice's excitement visibly faded. "Oh, I didn't actually *see* anything of him. I mean his cap was pulled down over his forehead. If I saw him again with overalls and those glasses on I suppose I *might* recognize him, but I know I couldn't *swear* it was the same man—I mean I wouldn't like to." She gathered resistance to the possibility of having to appear as a witness. "After all, I only saw him for a second."

"It's quite obvious that my lady wife could not give the police any useful information," Eldred pronounced, hand raised to repel objections. His tone managed to convey that if he had been there he would have had no difficulty in identifying the man. "They must have obtained full descriptions from the bank staff who will have had ample opportunity to look at the robbers."

Gregory, who had quietly taken the newspaper from Clarice's fluttering hand and was glancing through the story, looked up. "No, you're wrong there. While they were in the bank they wore masks as well as gloves."

"That may be so." Eldred was in no way put out. "However, there must have been dozens of people about at that time in the morning who saw all four of them when they arrived to put up the ladders, and the bank messenger must have some idea of the appearance of the men who asked to use the lavatory." He peered at the paper in Gregory's hand. "In any case, this is Friday's paper. How do we know that the police haven't already got them all in custody?"

"How indeed?" Basil agreed with a smile.

"If I was you I'd keep my trap shut," Perce advised Clarice. "They don't know as you knows anything—and, come to that, you don't know all that much. You don't want to have to pop back to London just to tell 'em that."

"You're absolutely right, Mr. Strongitharm," Eldred affirmed, taking his wife's arm with consequential decision. "Come along, dear. Oh, Juan," he called to the latter who was now behind the bar, "all right for the little boat tomorrow if it's fine? Right; then have it ready for us at ten."

He had almost reached the doorway when Bill Eddow, coming in, stopped short with a look of astonishment. "Good lord! Fancy seeing you—"

"We have a bungalow here," Eldred said curtly. Frowning, he watched Clarice take Bill's hand; then, with a brusque nod, he propelled her outside.

As they walked away she broke the uncomfortable silence. "You weren't very nice, dear. You should have shaken hands. He's done nothing wrong. I do think you should remember him—"

"I have no intention of doing so," he overrode her angrily.

"There's another matter I've been thinking about," she said after a pause. "I want to leave Colin something outright." When he made no reply she went on, "I thought ten thousand pounds."

"Ten thousand—umph. Well, if that is your wish, dear, you can trust me to see that he gets it—in the unlikely event of my surviving you."

22

Clarice knew her husband very much better than he suspected. He would not intend to break his word, but it was not in his character easily to part with money. "I'd like to say so in my will," she said.

"Very well. Then you can add a codicil tomorrow." His tone was such that she said no more.

Thersie left the bar immediately after the Pooles. She felt the need of fresh air before going to bed. Wistfully she thought that no one was likely to leave her a substantial legacy. Walking down to the beach, she stood for a few minutes listening to the night music of the sea, watching the lights of a coastal vessel move slowly northwards. Sitting down, leaning against a rock, she began to think about the man who had asked her to marry him, whom she had accepted and later had gently and unhappily told that she had changed her mind. It had not been because she did not like him; but liking alone was insufficient for marriage. She had not, she told herself, yet experienced love. Perhaps she never would. Perhaps she was incapable of love.

She became aware that two people were approaching and, unless they changed their course, would pass directly behind her. She recognized the voices. Consciously she tried to close her ears to their conversation; but, as they came nearer, she found it impossible not to overhear part of what they were discussing.

". . . the outline and your pencil notes," James was saying. "I think that should be enough to go ahead on."

Of Gregory's murmured reply only the word 'alternatives' was audible.

"Not good enough," she heard James say. "We'll sleep on it and have another talk tomorrow. But it seems to me a situation to which the answer is 'Let the Lord decide.' I'm off to bed now. Good night." Sand crunched crisply as he went up the beach.

Thersie returned to her thoughts. Some time later she jumped up, shook the sand out of her sandals and made her way to the bungalow.

Basil left the bar shortly after James went off with Gregory. Back in his sitting-room he looked up the time of the train he was to meet at Flassá and, after re-reading the telegram which Carmen had given him, tore it up into small pieces.

He had tried to persuade James to make an early night of it. James, however, had said that he had not seen Gregory for a long time and wanted a chat with him, promising that he would keep it brief. James had been as good as his word and was in his own bungalow within a quarter of an hour, sitting at his desk. He found himself in an indecisive frame of mind. If he now drafted the letter he wished to send tomorrow, it would be something off his chest. On the other hand, it might be best to have a word with Basil first. He pushed the typewriter aside. Glancing at the orange folder that held the first half of the manuscript of his book, he gave a weary shrug. A night's sleep was the best remedy— if he were able to sleep. Opening a desk drawer, he hesitated; then, taking out a blue folder, he went into the bedroom.

In the small hours he got out of bed and went into the kitchen to make a cup of tea. While the water heated, he recalled his meeting that afternoon with Miss Clegg and the kindly but positive tone of voice in which she had said, "If one refuses to go beyond facts, James, one doesn't often get as far as facts."

After James left him, Gregory continued to walk for some time; then, returning to the bar, he asked Juan for a whisky and soda. Upstairs he could hear a bath filling and the clop of Carmen's sandals as she tripped along the passage. Except for Beryl, Millie, and Cyril, the bar was now empty. Soon Beryl rose, whispered to Millie and, taking Cyril by the hand, led him out.

Forlornly Millie nursed the last inch of liquid in her glass. For a short time Gregory sat watching thoughtfully; then, going over to her table, he suggested that she have a final drink with him.

"I'm glad to find you alone," he said.

"Are you?" Millie's tone conveyed that previous opportunities had not been lacking.

"More than glad." He looked directly into her eyes. "I've been working hard on a story—and when I'm doing that I'm blind to the rest of the world."

"Are you writing a film?"

"No, a book. But I've written quite a number of film scripts." Suddenly he grinned. "Are you going to ask me if I can get you a film test?"

"And if I did?" she asked pertly.

"I'd say no. Not that you're not pretty enough for films. In fact you're the most attractive girl I've seen for a long time. I could take you to places where you'd be seen by producers and directors, and I could put you in the way of applying for crowd work. But I've never asked anyone to give a friend a film test. Producers don't welcome suggestions from unimportant people like writers. So please don't ask me."

"I wasn't going to," Millie said truthfully. Like many pretty girls without qualifications or any particular aptitude she had already done a little crowd work, and had realized that the step from anonymity to stardom is not made by uncrossing one's legs. She had received suave proposals and turned them down. To her, sex was something to enjoy with the partner of one's choice. Mutual attraction was the first essential, and to Millie that had come with gratifying frequency. Gregory, she had thought from the moment she saw him, would make a satisfying and satisfied bedmate. At last he had taken notice of her, and in Millie's mind, as she sipped at her second whisky, there could be no doubt about his intentions. But when—and how? Millie smiled to herself. That was one part of the unspoken purpose that, in her code, must be left to the man.

The ensuing conversation showed that Gregory was not without a plan. Millie giggled happily. She was still giggling when Gregory steered her through the deserted hall and left her at the door of the bedroom which she shared with Beryl.

Turning on the bed-light, Carmen opened *No End of a*

World. She was deeply engrossed when Juan came upstairs. As soon as he entered the bedroom she knew from his breathing that he was in a quarrelsome mood.

"What was in that packet Eldred gave you?" he demanded.

"Scent, Molyneux Cinq. The bottle's on the dressing-table."

"I won't have you accepting presents from him."

"What d'you expect me to do? Shove it back into his hand and tell him 'No, thanks'?" She closed the book. "If you don't like him giving me something, tell him yourself." She refrained from adding that the bottle was the smallest that Molyneux offered to the public.

He glowered and, snatching it up, went over to the window and threw it out. It fell soundlessly. Carmen smiled to herself. The bottle was almost certainly unbroken, and she had not removed the seal from the stopper.

"You behave like a whore," he told her angrily. "Kissing people and letting them stroke your backside."

"I kiss the people I like. I don't like Eldred—it's him that kisses me." She shuddered. "God, I wish he'd kiss you, then you'd know what it's like."

"You looked as if you were enjoying it."

"And what d'you expect me to do?" she snapped. "Spit in his face?"

"Keep on your side of the counter," he said curtly, "and don't behave as if you were waiting to jump into bed. I'm warning you. Don't let me see you kissing that old ram again or I'll do something about it."

"Oh, shut up." Carmen banged the book down on the bedside table. "Try and behave like a man and not like some bloody gangster in a film." She rolled over. "And if you think there's anything doing tonight, you've got another think coming."

26

3

Monday,
11th September

THE MORNING broke warm and windless. By half past seven a slight dawn mist had cleared, leaving a baby-blue sky across which sailed clouds like fistfuls of kapok. The sea was, as Eldred, looking out of the window, announced, like a looking-glass.

In the hotel the 'Phoebus Abroad' party straggled in to breakfast at the centre table. Soon Bill Eddow wandered in and, glancing round, remarked, "Everyone here except Millie. You'd better tell her to hurry up, Beryl."

"She won't be coming," said Beryl. "She says she doesn't feel so good, and she's going to stay in bed."

Gregory looked up from the corner table where he ate alone. "Sorry to hear that. Probably too much sun." He finished his cup of coffee and rose. "Enjoy your romp among the ruins." He smiled at Miss Clegg. "You can tell me all about it this evening."

Millie was sitting up when Beryl came in with a small bottle. "What have you got there?"

"Some capsule things. You're supposed to take one every four hours. You don't really need them, do you?"

"I've got a bit of a headache—honest, Beryl. And my tummy feels funny."

"What you've got is ants in your pants," Beryl said succinctly. "If you think I can't see as far as the next house, you're barmy."

27

"Honest, I'm not feeling so good. Give me one of those things and bring me a glass of water, will you?"

"O.K." Beryl watched her take one of the pink and white capsules and wash it down. "With what I think you're going to get up to you don't want to be loose," she commented dispassionately. "Why don't you give up mucking around? Don't you ever want to get married?"

"Yes, I do. I want a nice house and a couple of kids," Millie replied candidly. "But I've not found the boy I'd like to stick to forever."

"You're going a funny way about it, then. What fellow's going to marry a girl who offers it on a plate?"

"If he's the chap I want and he wants me he's not going to get it till we're out of the registry office. Till then I'm going to have my bit of fun. Why shouldn't I?" It was, Millie decided, her turn to attack. "I can't see what you find in a length of starched string like Cyril."

Beryl chuckled. "I'm getting the starch out of him. He's got a clean mind and a nice job in a bank with a good pension at the end. He's steady and he wants a family and," she finished with determination, "I'm not going to let him get away."

"He's a virgin, isn't he?"

"He'll get over that. Maybe we'll fumble at the start, but with a double bed and a bit of practice I reckon we'll make out all right." As she turned to go she enquired, "Want any food brought up to you."

"No, I think I'm best on an empty stomach."

"Well, you ought to know." Beryl cackled and was gone.

"That's the lot." Perce laid the Nikonos underwater camera carefully on the car seat. "We'd better get a move on, Jack, if we're going to finish this morning."

After a twenty-minute drive they reached the beginning of a track where a sandy-haired man was sitting on a stone, whittling a piece of wood with a penknife.

"Morning, Bob," they called. "Everything ready?"

"It's been ready this past half-hour." He helped them to

take the diving equipment from the car and, lumping a fair share of the gear, led the way down a steep incline. "Had a fellow around last night," he called back. "Seemed interested in what he could see and asked if he could come out with me some time. Told him I was off home today."

"Nosey?" asked Jack laconically.

"Not partic'ly. Asked what I was doing, and I said I had a couple of pals taking pictures. Mind the next yard or two. Rock's splitting away."

Sweating and in silence they came to an inlet where a thirty-foot boat lay. Once aboard they rested for a short time; then Bob started the engine and put out to sea. Fifteen minutes later they reached a marking buoy north-east of Cap Tabal.

"How long d'you reckon to be?" Bob asked.

"Not more 'n thirty minutes the first time and, if we have to go down again, another fifteen or twenty." Perce eased himself into a neoprene suit.

Jack spat into a mask and rubbed his hand round the face plate. "Got the lifting bags handy, Bob?"

Bob grunted, gesturing in the direction of a waterproof sheet that covered a portable compressor.

Soon Perce was fastening his aqualung harness and checking the quick release. He watched Jack test his air valve and take several breaths; then, signing to Bob, he lumbered over to a ladder lashed to the gunwale.

They were rubbing themselves down after the second dive when Bob mentioned that two boats had approached while they were in the water. "Shouted and signalled to them to sheer off—and they did. Looked like holiday folk to me."

Two hours passed before the three men climbed for the last time up to the parked car.

"If you tell me again that this ruddy compressor only weighs a hundred pounds I'll drop my end on your foot," panted Bob.

"Might be a bit over the odds, come to think of it." Perce winked at Jack. "Wouldn't surprise me if Bob didn't let out all that heavy air when he charged them bottles."

At nine o'clock Basil locked the door of his bungalow and went over to his car. Like all the other bungalows except one, it was flanked by a car port composed of six metal poles with cross-pieces forming a frame across which pine branches had been laid and secured by short lengths of wire. The exception was the Pooles' bungalow, to which Eldred had added a garage built of brick, with a concrete strip leading to the banjo.

This morning Basil was grimly thoughtful. He had considered looking in on James but, seeing that curtains were still drawn across the windows, decided not to. Across the bay he observed a somewhat dilapidated mini-bus standing outside the hotel. The tour party was about to embark. Miss Clegg, in trousers and sporting an age-yellowed Panama hat, carried a large leather bag and the notebook without which she was seldom seen. The remainder clutched a selection of brightly coloured beach-bags. Bill Eddow, leaning against the radiator, was having a word with the driver. Subconsciously, Basil noted the absence of Millie's fair head. Getting into the car and proceeding cautiously to the main road, he drove for some minutes before stopping at a petrol station. There he chatted with the owner while the latter filled the tank. Then, opening his wallet, he found that he had left his main stock of money behind.

"Trust me to pay you next time?" he asked.

"Pay me when you like." The owner laughed. "A rogue always knows an honest man."

James had slept badly. It was nearly ten o'clock before he got out of bed. He was drawing back the sitting-room curtains when Thersie's car passed the Bar Felix and turned up the dirt road. Presently, in shirt and bathing shorts, carrying a rolled-up air mattress, a sun umbrella and a beach bag containing a towel, an Eric Ambler thriller, a notebook and a couple of apples, he came out to find the bay deserted.

The cleft that led to the smaller bay was even narrower than he had remembered it. The little beach, too, seemed to have shrunk. It was strange, James reflected, how memory magnified, how one recalled the houses of one's childhood as being so much larger than they were, and the school holidays as times of never-ending sunshine. At what stage of life did reality overtake one? No, not reality, but actuality. For reality was a personal interpretation of what had happened. Actuality was what had in fact taken place: often something one preferred to ignore or forget or, by applying a rose-coloured gloss, to transmute into what one was prepared to acknowledge.

He opened the umbrella and, pushing the shaft into the sand, sat down to blow up the air mattress. Soon he lay down to read, and very soon the book dropped from his hand and he dozed. When he awoke, the sea beckoned and, swimming out a short distance, he turned on his back and, eyes closed, considered the problem that clouded the future. Some time later he became mistily aware that he was not alone in the water. He was about to turn over when hands gripped his head.

In the Pooles' bungalow no one could doubt that the daily maid, Asunción, had arrived. Clarice, at the desk in the sitting-room, heard the crockery clash on the marble draining-board.

Eldred had some time ago returned to the bedroom to select his wardrobe for the morning's outing. Clarice gazed at the sheet of paper onto which she had carefully copied out half a dozen opening lines. She found herself recalling the days of Eldred's courtship. He had then been studying accountancy. Her own substantial private means would allow them to marry and live in comfort until he passed the final examination. Then, six months after the wedding, a bachelor uncle had died suddenly and Eldred had inherited a considerable fortune. Whatever desire he might have had to earn a living faded away. He bought a house in the country where they lived conventional and childless lives until, in his forties, Eldred was seized with an urge to travel. A tour of Spain had led them, by a misreading of the map—or, as Eldred insisted, by an error on the part of the map-maker—to Cala Felix, with which place Clarice had fallen in love, buying on the spot one of the three bungalows which were then being erected. Here Eldred had up to the present been content to spend two or three months of the year.

This year a return to London for a month had been necessitated by Clarice's loss of her top dental plate, sneezed out as she flushed the cistern in a restaurant cloakroom. She passed a tongue exploringly round her new plates and, with a start, brought back her mind to the present task. Picking up her pen, she began to write. She had put down only a few words when she heard Eldred stepping smartly along the passage. Snatching up the sheet and opening a drawer already stuffed with papers, she pushed it down on top of the pile and rammed the drawer home.

Eldred did not ask the question she had anticipated. Instead he said briskly, "Five to ten, my dear. Time to be off." He sniffed. "Something's burning."

"Not now," she assured him hastily. "I—I put a cigarette down on some paper and it caught alight, but I managed to get it to the fireplace in time."

Eldred glanced at the small heap of ashes in the purely ornamental hearth with which the architect had endowed each of the bungalows. "It's out," he informed her as if she were unlikely to have checked this fact for herself. "Are those the clothes you're going in, or have you still got to change?"

"Only my shoes." She trotted off to the bedroom.

"Have you made sure that Asunción will lock up when she leaves?" he asked fussily on her return.

"She always does, and leaves the key with Carmen." Clarice followed him across the terrace and onto the beach. Watching him bend over the outboard motor, she prayed that it would start before he had fidgeted it into obstinate immobility. It fired; and they were heading out into the bay when she heard a shout. Juan was leaning out of his bedroom window, signalling with a pyjama'd arm. What he called she could not hear. She waved back.

They were approaching the entrance to La Caleta on their

return journey when the engine stuttered, then picked up again.

"I do think our friends could have asked us to stay to lunch," Eldred said. There was a note of querulousness in his voice.

"I'm sure they would if I hadn't mentioned that Colin might turn up at any time," Clarice replied placatingly. From the moment of their arrival she had realized that Eldred's acquaintances were not particularly pleased to see them. Eldred had remained impervious to the obvious, and it had required all her tact to persuade him to leave before the situation became embarrassing.

Once more the engine stuttered, picked up, stuttered again and died.

"What's happened?" she asked.

"Looks as if we've run out of fuel," Eldred barked peevishly. "These blasted Spaniards, letting us go out without checking. I'll let Juan know what I think of him." He picked up one of the two paddles. "I'm not going to take the boat all the way back. We'll put in here, and Juan can come and fetch her." He held out the paddle. "Here, you take this."

Clarice screamed.

"What on earth's the matter, dear? Nothing to be frightened of."

"Look." She pointed. "There's someone drowning over there."

A pair of legs thrashed the surface. A goggled swimmer seemed to be making a desperate effort to hold the drowning person's head. Eldred bent and scrabbled for the second paddle which was just out of reach. "Dig into the water as hard as you can," he panted to Clarice. "I'll keep her straight."

When next they looked up only the goggled swimmer was in sight and coming fast towards them. In a moment strong hands grabbed the dinghy amidships. It tipped dangerously.

"Hi," shouted Eldred. "You'll have us over."

The swimmer appeared not to hear, but heaved again, dropped back and heaved once more. Eldred bellowed. The next moment he and Clarice were in the water. Clarice clung to the bows as the boat began slowly to drift shorewards. Where was Eldred? The boat swung slightly round. The goggled swimmer surfaced, gulping in air, then turned towards Clarice.

At eleven o'clock Bill Eddow emerged from the hotel. Juan was waiting by the launch and kept him talking for a time before helping him aboard, handing over a petrol can and calling out a final instruction.

Bill was some miles out and taking the launch in a wide circle when he saw a ship in the distance and recognized her as the MS *Cellini* on her regular run from Marseilles to Barcelona, from where she would continue to Greece and the eastern Mediterranean. From a porthole aft a hand waved a red cloth. Bill raised both arms and waved back. From the porthole what looked like a child's orange playball dropped into the water. Opening the throttle, Bill made towards it. By the time he had scooped it aboard the *Cellini* was a rapidly diminishing hull. He turned southwards, putting on speed as he passed the Cabo de Sebastián and came in sight of Llafranch.

One o'clock struck as he sat outside a café, sipping a second glass of beer and looking round at the occupants of the other sun-umbrella'd tables. A bulging brown-paper shopping bag rested on the chair beside him. People were drifting in, and soon every table had been taken. He glanced up and nodded as a corpulent man with a polite *"Permiso?"* sat down on the opposite chair and fanned himself with a folded copy of the *Vanguardia*. Bill took out a tobacco pouch, filled his pipe and, lighting it, put the match-box on the table.

"Excuse me, *señor*." The fat man picked up the box. "I see there is a picture of a blue Persian cat on your box. My granddaughter is collecting this series of cats. I wonder if you would be good enough to exchange your box for mine." He smiled. "I have used only one match, so I shall not be robbing you."

"Of course." Bill accepted the proffered partly-open box and put it in his pocket.

34

The fat man smiled again. "A fortunate meeting," he said. "Perhaps you would care to have this *Vanguardia*. I have finished with it."

Shortly, Bill paid the bill, exchanged goodbyes, tucked the paper under his arm and went down to the launch. Boarding it, he saw that an envelope had been placed by the wheel. It was addressed to Juan Carosco. Evidently someone had recognized Juan's boat.

Fastening the clip at the side of her bikini, Millie adjusted the scrap of material over her hips. With a stir of anticipation she smiled at her reflection in the looking-glass. The headache, together with the slight queasiness in her stomach, had passed not long after Beryl had given her the capsule, and the little bottle was in the bag with her lipstick and powder. She looked again at her watch. It was five past twelve. Gregory would be waiting for her.

Picking up beach-towel and bag, she opened the door. There was no one in sight. Her rubber-soled sandals made no noise as she crossed the hall. That too was empty, and she did not see Escipión at his desk in the small office behind the reception counter. Reaching Gregory's room, she tapped on the door and slipped in.

Gregory was by the window. "Stay where you are for a moment," he said quietly, as he pulled a cord to angle the slats of the Venetian blind more steeply. The light in the room dimmed. "Mustn't let anyone see us." He smiled down at the upturned face. "You look wonderful."

"I didn't really feel so good first thing, so I took one of the capsules Beryl gave me. I've brought them with me just in case—"

"Better take another one now." His eyes twinkled. "We don't want to be interrupted, do we? Here, give me the bottle and I'll get a glass of water." Releasing her, he went into the bathroom, returning in a few moments. He watched her drain the glass and slipped the bottle back into her handbag. "Better go on taking them until you're sure," he advised, picking her up and laying her down gently on the double bed. Then he was beside her, and it was with a rush of joy that she felt the hands of experience pass over her body.

She woke as his hand fell on her. He was lying on his back and snoring very, very quietly. As she moved his arm across her belly she felt him stir. She was about to kiss him when a sudden qualm came into her mind. "How long have we been asleep?" she whispered. "I mustn't be here when the others come back."

"It can't be late," he murmured reassuringly. "I only dozed off for a second or two. Look at your watch—or there's a clock beside you."

Through half-open eyes she glanced at her wrist-watch. "Oh, it's only twenty past one—nearly twenty five past on the clock." She turned to meet his lips. "Oh, Greg," were the only words either uttered until he leaned across her to pick up the clock and say sadly, "It's just after four, Millie. We'll have to get up. We both need a shower. You use the bathroom first."

"I don't want to move," she said drowsily.

"Then I'll have to carry you." He smiled down at the pretty, glistening face and, unstrapping her wrist watch, kissed her, rolled out of bed and picked her up.

When at last she had combed her hair and put on fresh lipstick he opened the door and looked out. "All clear," he told her.

She made no move. "When can we do it again, Greg?"

"The next time everyone's out of the hotel and there's no one to see you coming here." He looked out again. "Still clear. Don't forget to take another of the capsules when you get back to your room." He patted her behind as she went out.

She was lying on her bed when Beryl came in shortly after five o'clock and picked up the little bottle that Millie had put on the dressing-table. "Taken three of these things, I see."

"Yes, I feel ever so much better."

Beryl scanned her friend's face and giggled. "I bet you do. Doesn't need a doctor to see that that's not the only medicine you've had."

Turning into the station yard at Flassá, Basil braked with
a scatter of grit and, jumping out, ran past the two parked
taxis into the waiting-room. It was empty. Going onto the
platform, he glanced at the clock. As usual, it was out of
order. Then, turning left, he saw the two suitcases, an old
green one and the new dark red wardrobe case which he had
given her on her birthday. So she had arrived—and was
waiting for him. But where? As he asked the question she
came out of the shabby little *cantina*.

He tore along the platform and took her in his arms. "I'm
so sorry, darling. I had a wretched job to do this morning
and got held up. I'll tell you about it later. Are you all
right?"

There was such concern in his face and voice that Antonia
could only melt. "I was just on the point of spending two or
three pounds on a taxi. I'm glad I waited." She gazed at him
closely. "You look harassed."

"I'm not now." He collected the suitcases, and they went
to the car. "What sort of journey did you have?"

"Dirty and boring. I wish I had the courage to fly, but the
take-off and the landing frighten me."

"Nothing else does, darling."

"Not when I'm with you." She put her hand lightly on his
as they sat down in the car. "I was wishing in the train that
our partnership weren't over."

"The particular job's over and finished with as far as
we're concerned," he said, "but not the partnership—at least
not unless you say 'no'."

She stared ahead, a half-smile on her lips. "Is that a pro-
posal of marriage?" she said at last.

"I put it badly—too many negatives. But that's what it
was, Antonia."

"And the answer's 'yes' and 'yes'—and 'yes' again."
There was a catch in her voice. "I've been waiting a long
time."

"I'd have asked you a hundred times, dearest, if it hadn't

been for—for the sword of Damocles."

"Even if the sword had been falling I'd have said 'yes'."
She paused. "This will be our honeymoon."

He chuckled happily. "A little unconventional to have the
honeymoon before the wedding."

"The wedding doesn't matter, Basil."

"It does. You're going to make an honest man of me
whether you like it or not. Damn it all, a respectable solicitor can't live in sin." He braked and drew into the side of the
road. "I've got something for you." He gave her a small tissue-wrapped packet and watched her open it.

"A wedding ring." She turned it round and round as if it
were an object she had never seen before.

"I thought you should choose the engagement ring yourself."

"We'll have the honeymoon first." Happily, slowly, carefully, as if it might vanish at her touch, she slipped the ring
onto her finger. "I suppose I oughtn't to wear it. Everyone
will think that you've got someone else's wife staying with
you."

Basil grinned. "To hell with everyone—except us."

"Anyone around? There's a couple of blokes here with
their tongues hanging out."

Carmen recognized Perce's hoarse shout. "Help yourselves," she called from the kitchen. "I'll be along in a mo."
Coming into the bar, she saw the car outside, the roof rack
piled with luggage over which a tarpaulin had been roped.
"Not leaving, are you?" she asked in surprise.

"Just popping south to have a look round. We'll be back
Wednesday. Bungalow's locked. Take care of the key, will
you, love?"

"You two look as if you were up to some mischief."

"Not us." Jack's tone was one of shocked virtue. "Them
days was over long since, wasn't they, Perce?"

"Too long. Can't go mucking around now we're fam'ly
men." Perce emptied his glass. "Got to be off now." He
pushed coins across the counter.

"Don't do anything I wouldn't do," Carmen called after them.

"You tell us what you wouldn't do if you got the chance!" Perce called back.

Reaching the top of the rise, Colin Dennison stopped and took a deep breath. Before him, and below several folds in the scrub-covered hills, lay a bay and a dozen or so white-washed bungalows. On the right of the bay stood a two-storey building on the flat roof of which lines of washing hung in the windless air. So this, he thought, is Cala Felix. Aunt Clarice was right—it was beautiful. It was also deserted. The sole sign of human life was a long estate-car outside one of the bungalows.

To the right of the larger building a promontory pointed a rocky finger out to sea. A small white boat was approaching it from the south. He could hear the beat of the outboard motor. There were two people in the boat, a man and a woman in a pink dress; but they were too far away for their faces to be distinguishable.

Moving on, he followed a path that led to a clump of pines in the next dip. Shortly, a cove to the right of the promontory came into sight. There was a bather in the narrow inlet, some twenty yards out and floating face upwards. Near the mouth of what looked like a cleft in the rocks, an air-mattress lay half under a striped sun umbrella planted in the sand. Beside the umbrella were two towels; but there was no sign of any other person than the solitary bather, unless what seemed to be a slight extension of shadow was that of someone stooped under the blue and white umbrella.

With Colin's next step the cove went out of sight behind the tops of the pine-trees. Reaching their shade, he un-buckled his rucksack and sat down to eat some biscuits and a banana. After some fifteen minutes he re-shouldered the rucksack and began to climb the next rise. As he breasted the summit, the cove once again came into view—and abruptly he stopped, mind alerted, breath momentarily held.

Mind and heart were racing as he stood later, gasping for

breath, on the patch of sand beside the striped umbrella. In the inlet a narrow-beamed white dinghy with an outboard motor rolled sluggishly, half-submerged.

Shading his eyes, he turned full circle. His stance, the clenching of the other hand, the jerky movement of the head, indicated question and apprehension. He turned again, scanning each inch of the surroundings. There was no one to be seen. Nothing stirred. Only the harsh wailing of a pair of wheeling gulls broke the early afternoon silence.

For a few moments he stood tensely; then, reaching a decision, he moved fast, making for the base of the promontory and clambering over the rocks. At a fissure he came to a sudden halt. Beneath his feet was the body of a woman, the torn skirt of a sodden pink dress rucked up to her thighs. She lay prone, face half-immersed in the shallow water, one arm underneath her, the other stretched past her head as if she were pointing to something she could not see.

Lowering himself rapidly, he lifted the body and turned it in his arms. The face that gazed blankly upwards was a face he knew well—the face of his Aunt Clarice.

His seeking fingers could find no pulse, nor could he detect any sign of breathing. Carrying her to the beach, he laid her down on the air mattress. It was more than eight years since the school swimming instructor had taught his class the Holger-Nielsen method of artificial respiration, and then Colin had practised it on living cooperative youngsters. Now he must keep calm and recall what he had learned. Opening her mouth, he took out a strand of sea-weed and, after a brief hesitation, the double set of false teeth. Spreading out the towel that lay nearby, he placed her on it face down, head towards the sea so that the slope of the beach should bring it below the level of her feet. Bending her elbows so that one wrist lay on the other, he turned her head sideways to rest on the topmost wrist. Then, kneeling before her, he spread his hands across her back and with straightened arms pressed down. Rock backwards, he muttered to himself, take the elbows, lift and lower. Complete the cycle and repeat, repeat, repeat. . . .

40

He did not hear the car draw up on the road above; he did not know that anyone had come until the girl knelt beside him. Automatically he obeyed what she said, helped her to turn the body and watched her press the head back, close the mouth, blow gently but firmly up the nose, glance at the chest and blow again. A long time passed before she sat up, swaying a little. "I'm afraid she's dead," she said hoarsely. "Can you go on doing exactly what I've been doing while I fetch a doctor? Do it now—at once."

Again, without question, he obeyed.

She went on, "There's no telephone here, but I know where the nearest call box is. I may have to fetch the doctor myself, but I'll be as quick as possible."

He gestured understanding and heard her running to the road, then the whirr of a starter motor. Her absence seemed interminable, his efforts unavailing; but he was still trying to blow life into the inanimate body when cars drew up above and two uniformed men and a civilian carrying a leather bag followed Thersie as she hurried towards him.

A little later the doctor rose from his knees and shook his head. "I can do nothing, *Teniente*," he said.

The Civil Guard officer shrugged regretfully. "Does any-one know who she is?" he queried.

Colin realized that the question was directed at the girl and himself, but his few words of Spanish were insufficient for understanding. He gestured non-comprehension.

She repeated the question in English. "Shall I translate?" she asked.

"Please," Colin said gratefully, and gave her the reply, ad-ding his own name. She relayed the answer.

"You speak excellent Spanish." The *Teniente* eyed her ap-preciatively. "Then she and *Señor* Dennison were together?"

Colin said no. He had found her on the rocks. He pointed to the spot near which, like a marker buoy, the half-sub-merged boat now swayed slowly.

The *Teniente* listened without comment to Colin's story; then, "And you, *señorita*?" he asked.

"My name is Sallis, Thersie Sallis," she replied. "I'm

staying in one of the bungalows in Cala Felix." She told him how she was driving back from San Feliu de Guíxols when she saw the empty, water-logged boat drifting in the inlet, stopped and ran down to see if help were needed. "I'm trained in first aid and could see I had to act at once, so I took over from Mr Dennison. When I realized there was little hope I went for a doctor and, as you know, he telephoned you."

The *Teniente* picked up the beach bag, took out a notebook and read what was on the cover. "This apparently belonged to a *Señor* Rowley. Who is he?"

"A writer staying in one of the bungalows."

With an abrupt apology Colin interrupted. "I must find my uncle and tell him what's happened." He looked at Thersie for help. "Can you show me his bungalow?"

"A moment, please." The *Teniente* spoke with authority. "It seems probable that *Señor* Dennison's aunt was in that boat and had an accident. Would she have been in it alone?"

"I don't think so," Colin said slowly. "She couldn't have managed an outboard motor, but she might have used a paddle."

Thersie translated.

"There are two paddles in the sea," the *Teniente* observed. In the ensuing silence he turned to the other uniformed man who had remained attentive in the background. "Go to Cala Felix and find out whether *Señor* Poole and *Señor* Rowley are there. If they are not, then we must envisage that the accident involved one or both of them. Bring back everyone who can dive." His eyes returned to Colin and Thersie. "Is there anything else that either of you can tell me?"

James, she said, had mentioned last night that he planned to spend the day at La Caleta. "I also heard Mr Poole arranging to borrow the boat." They were still answering questions when the Civil Guard reappeared, squeezing through the cleft. He was followed by Escipión, Gregory and Bill and, almost immediately, by Basil, Antonia and Juan.

It was an hour, a long, long, nervous hour before the bodies of James and Eldred were brought ashore.

The *Teniente*'s office was small, and the walls almost completely concealed by steel filing-cabinets. The sole window was closed. "I am assuming for the moment," he said to Thersie, "that these three people died after some accident. I gathered from *Señor* Seaton that, although *Señor* Rowley was a good swimmer, he was recovering from a serious illness. Were *Señor* and *Señora* Poole good swimmers?"

Thersie translated, then gave Colin's reply. "My uncle was not a strong swimmer, and my aunt a very poor one."

"Were they both in good health?"

"They seemed so when I saw them last month."

"You understand that there will have to be autopsies, and that the burials must take place within forty-eight hours unless the deceaseds' relatives wish for burial in England."

"So far as I know," said Colin, "I am my uncle and aunt's only close relation."

"They have no parents or children living?"

"No. And my aunt was my late mother's only sister. I believe my uncle was an only child. His mother married a second time and lived abroad. I remember my uncle saying that she was dead. He didn't mention any children."

The *Teniente* made notes, then put down his pen. "If you wish them to be buried in England I suggest you telephone your Consul in Barcelona now. You may use the telephone in the next room."

"And Mr Rowley's burial?" queried Thersie.

"Perhaps someone knows who his relatives are and how to get in touch with them."

"His friend Mr Seaton will probably know. I'll ask him," she volunteered.

The *Teniente* rose, made a formal expression of his sympathy and shook hands. At the doorway he gave instructions that they should be taken to the telephone.

"I think it would be best to have them buried here," Thersie said when they were alone. She explained the problems if they were to be taken to England.

"Embalmed." A picture of what that could involve decided Colin.

By the time they left the Cuartel darkness had fallen. They reached Cala Felix to find Basil beckoning from the doorway of his bungalow.

"Antonia's got supper for you. I've told Carmen not to expect you, Thersie, and I've got the key of your aunt's bungalow, Colin. But your rucksack's here, and if you'd like to have the spare bedroom you're more than welcome. You both look exhausted. Come along in and have a drink." James, he told them later, was a widower and had no children. "So I've taken it on myself to decide to have him buried here."

Later Colin walked with Thersie to her bungalow. He had decided to sleep in his aunt's bungalow where there was a bed already made up for him. But he was pleased when Thersie asked, "Would you like to come and have breakfast with me on the terrace? Eight thirty, then. Tea or coffee?"

"Coffee, please. And thank you for all your help, Thersie. I don't know how I would have managed without you." He stood for a moment awkwardly, said "Good night" and, before she could muster a reply, turned and was off.

4

Tuesday, 12ᵗʰ September and Wednesday morning, 13ᵗʰ September

Bᴵᴿᴰ sᴏɴɢ woke Colin at
seven. He showered, dressed and had made his bed before
remembering that his aunt had mentioned a daily maid.
Then he went into the sitting-room. On a shelf by the window stood a framed studio photograph of Clarice. It had
been taken before her marriage. She looked as if the bud of
her life was about to flower; expectant, waiting and watching
for the return of her young Lochinvar. But young Lochinvar
had not returned. He had found another bride, and she had
married Eldred. Colin had often wondered why. He had been
fond of his aunt. For his uncle he had not much cared. It was
not easy to like a man who liked himself too well.

Thersie was making coffee when he arrived. Her deep tan
was enhanced by a white blouse and shorts. Her smile of
welcome was unaffectedly warm. Breakfast had been laid on
the terrace table, and he noted with pleasure the egg cups at
each place and the delicious smell of toasting bread. Soon
they were sitting down and he was enjoying the first satisfying breakfast he had eaten since he left England.

"I'm teaching sociology at Manchester," he said some
time later in answer to her question. "I'm in line for a better
job in London—and there's a possibility of going to the
States."

"Which would mean uprooting yourself from everything
you have. Could you bear to do that?"

45

"I haven't got any ties. My father and mother are both dead—and I was the only child. So I'm free as air; no commitments of any kind." He picked up the cup of coffee which she had refilled. "Thank you, Thersie—that's a nice name. I've never heard it before."

"It's not really a name." She made a wry face. "I was christened Thermothis. It sounds like a kind of vacuum flask, doesn't it, or something to spray on clothes which you're putting away? Father chose it. He's an Egyptologist, and Thermothis is the Greek version of some Egyptian goddess whose name I've forgotten. It's an awful name to have. You can hardly say it without lisping, and when I write it people just can't believe I've spelled it right. I wish I'd been christened something ordinary like Jane or Mary."

"I prefer Thersie. It suits you."

"That's what Perce said." She laughed and described the brothers with lively amusement, stopping suddenly to say, "There's the maid Asunción going into your bungalow. Did you leave it unlocked? I'd lock it if I were you. There've been some gipsies around recently. Look, you'd better go along and see her. She'll know what happened, and she'll want to embrace you and cry for ten minutes. I'll come along and help you to talk to her—and, in any case, she'll want to know if she's to come every day while you're here. She cycles from her home a mile or so away." Thersie rose. "Shall we just take the breakfast things into the kitchen, and I'll lock up."

Asunción had sobbed a soul-satisfying dirge, had dried her eyes, been comforted and asked to continue coming for the present when Basil put his head round the door. "Am I interrupting?" he asked and, being assured that he wasn't, went on, "I wondered if I could help you in any way, Colin. You'll probably want to notify your uncle and aunt's solicitors and their bank. I'm going to send off wires to James' lawyer and bank, and I thought I could send yours at the same time."

Colin accepted the offer gratefully. "They both banked at

the Capital and Counties at Downchester. I don't know who their solicitors were, but the bank probably will."

"Is there anyone else you ought to let know?"

"No one, I think, except their housekeeper." Colin considered. "I'd be grateful if you would tell her that they have had a fatal accident, and say I'll be writing today and that I'll come and see her as soon as I can." He tore the top sheet from a block of writing-paper and wrote down the name and address.

"Got a black tie?" asked Basil. "Nor have I. I'll bring a couple back. Come and have lunch with us—say one thirty." With a friendly wave he was gone.

"Let's go and see Carmen," suggested Thersie. "She's offered to give me meals until my parents arrive, and I know she'll do the same for you. I must tell her we shan't need lunch. Asunción will leave the key at the bar when she's finished, and we can pick it up later." She looked up at the sun glowing in a cloudless sky. "You know," she said, "I don't think it would be heartless to bathe."

The long, hot day passed. By unspoken consent there was little discussion of yesterday's tragic events among the visitors who, superficially, behaved as if neither James nor the Pooles had ever existed. Millie was happy to find that Beryl and Cyril, instead of disappearing through the cleft, swam and sunbathed with her. Miss Clegg, leaning against her personal rock, filled a dozen pages of her note-book. The results would in due course appear in a series of articles on the teaching of children which had been commissioned by a well-known educational journal. Gregory, except for a short swim while the others lunched, could be heard at his typewriter until dusk. Bill, with nothing to do, did nothing observable until late afternoon when he took Carmen's children for a short spin in the launch. On the hotel terrace four substantial figures lay in motionless contemplation, bringing themselves to an upright stance only when the clatter of plates announced the approach of another meal-time.

Wednesday morning 13th September

The burial service was over shortly after eleven the following morning, and the Chaplain who had met the mourners at the sad little English cemetery at Palamós shook hands and drove back to Barcelona. It had been a small gathering. Carmen had come with Thersie and Colin; Basil and Antonia had taken Gregory and Miss Clegg who, alone of the 'Phoebus Abroad' party, wished to pay her last respects to the dead.

It was Gregory's suggestion, when they stopped to drop Carmen at the bar, that they went in for a drink. "I'd like to have some little memento of James," he mentioned some minutes later. "Do you think anyone would mind if I took something quite small like a book, perhaps one of his own novels?"

"I was going to ask the executors for something for myself," said Basil. "If there's any particular book you'd like I'll let them know. I'm quite sure they'll say 'yes'."

"That reminds me. I've got James's copy of *Fabled Shore*. It's signed by the author and is probably worth a pound or two," Miss Clegg broke in. "I think I'd better put it back in his shelves."

"Give it to me, then," said Carmen. "I've got the key and I'll return the book when I tidy up the place."

"I thought Asunción looked after his bungalow as well as after the Pooles'."

"So she did, Greg. But I don't want to let the key out of my hands until we know who's entitled to have it. I s'pose you wouldn't know, Basil?"

"Not the slightest idea. You'd better hold onto it until we hear from the lawyers. I expect they'll send someone here to settle matters. No, thanks, nothing more for me." He put a hand over his glass and caught Antonia's eye. Soon Miss Clegg and Gregory followed them out.

"If you two want a bite to eat, just pop along two-ish, Thersie," Carmen invited her remaining visitors. "There's enough and to spare. No—well, any time you want something you've only got to say." She watched them walk towards the Pooles' bungalow. They'll make a good pair, her matchmakers instinct whispered. Nice that he's taller than her.

In the hotel linen cupboard Montserrat and Teresa gossiped as they sorted and stacked the clean sheets. The inward-opening door was half closed, so that Gregory did not notice them as he passed to go to his room. They had nearly completed the job when a pair of sandalled feet pattered past. Montserrat peeped. "It's her," she breathed, "and in nothing but a bikini." They tittered.

"Come in," called Gregory from the bathroom as he heard the light knock. He had taken off the suit he had worn for the funeral and was bending over the basin in his jockey shorts. With a bare foot he pushed the door shut.

"It's me," said a voice he recognized. "I've brought back the rest of the medicine. I don't need any more."

"Good. Put the bottle down somewhere," he requested, turning on the shower taps. He sponged himself, towelled down briskly and came into the bedroom to find Millie looking at herself in the long mirror and smoothing back a lock of hair.

"Do you want something, Millie?"

"I haven't seen you all yesterday or today, Greg."

"And I haven't see you," he said regretfully. "But I was working hard yesterday, and I've got to get down to it again, my dear. And, Millie, you shouldn't come to my room at this time of day. Someone's bound to see you—and we don't want the whole hotel talking about you—about us. Look, leave it to me to think up a plan. You'd better go now. I'll see if the passage is clear."

"All right," she agreed meekly. "Just give me a kiss." She moved a step forward and raised her face.

The next moment she was pressed tightly against him, her hands locked behind his head, her body wriggling rhythmically. Oh, damn the girl, he exclaimed inwardly and tried to step back, only to find a heel jammed against his ankle. He pushed hard at her rib cage, and abruptly she fell back onto the bed. Somehow the metal clasp-ring at the side of her bikini came apart, and she lay there, hips bared.

What time passed neither knew. It was the light on her glossy skin that brought him realization that the blind was undrawn. But no one outside, he reassured himself, can see the bed. Holding a shirt before him, he drew the blind down, then went to the door and shot the bolt.

Later, much later, he put on a dressing-gown and opened the door. The passage was empty and the linen cupboard key hanging as usual on the hook on the door post. He beckoned and she slipped out. It was then that he noticed the little white bow on the back of the bikini. What was it that the bow reminded him of? Of course, the scut of a rabbit. A rabbit! "My god," he said aloud, "I need a bodyguard."

5

Wednesday afternoon,
13ᵗʰ September

A SMALL GREY car came along the road at a steady eighty kilometres an hour. The occupant drove with practised ease, his hands resting lightly on the steeringwheel. His face was well formed, the chin perhaps a trifle over-long. A faint smile of pleasure in the distant glimpse of the sea, in the sunshine, in the greenness of the landscape, disclosed white, even teeth. The jet-black hair was brushed to a fine polish, the cheeks seemed freshly shaved. The eyes were of an unusual shade of blue that was near to violet. A cream poplin shirt moulded to his chest by the breeze from the open windows evidenced a trimly muscular figure. On the back seat a jacket of cinnamon-coloured linen lay carefully folded.

At first sight one might have guessed this man to be a lawyer, banker or administrator—and one would have been right in thinking him a professional man. His name was Salvador Borges, and he was an Inspector in the Brigade of Criminal Investigation, who—as on many previous occasions—had, because of his admirable English and his long acquaintance with English people both in their own country and in Spain, been invited to inquire into the possibility of murder at Cala Felix. He was also a husband of recent standing whose young wife Benita would in less than three months time bear him a child—they had little doubt it would be a son. Would the boy, he wondered, have the russet hair

51

and clear skin of Benita's Scottish parents? He glanced at the seat beside him where his dog Shadow, a slim Bedlington terrier like a quicksilver lamb, sat, nose half out of window, sniffing eagerly at the varied smells blown into the car. Shadow's ears quivered, but she did not move. She was the perfect female passenger, receptive, acceptant and silent.

A roadside sign indicated that he was approaching a petrol station, and he began to slow down. Shortly, he drew up beside a row of pumps. A white-overalled man was filling the tank of a dark-green car with a G.B. plate on the boot. "Up to the top as usual?" he asked a tall, nearly bald man with a scar above his left ear, who leaned against the coachwork.

"Please." The tall man watched the petrol gushing into the tank and, as the flow ceased, looked at the pump dial. "That's forty litres today, plus the forty you let me have on Monday morning. How much for topping up the battery?"

"Me charge a friend for water?" The overalled man, who was also the owner, spat expressively as he screwed on the tank cap. "For the petrol a thousand pesetas—the price is up again." As he took the bank-note he noticed the bright orange mercurochrome on the last two fingers of his customer's left hand. "You have hurt yourself!" he exclaimed.

"Nothing fatal. Just a scratch." Basil got into the car, smiled goodbye and drove off.

"*Un buen amigo,*" the garageman observed as he brought the petrol hose over to the Inspector's car. "He comes every year and he brings me toys from England for the children." He went on chatting while he filled the tank and checked the oil level on the dipstick. It was impossible not to talk to a man who listened with such genuine interest and who seemed not to have heard about the three foreigners drowned at La Caleta. There was a rumour, he mentioned, that the deaths had not been accidental. The customer prompted, but learned little more.

After some kilometres the grey car turned onto a dirt road, slowed to a crawl as it met the potholes, passed the Bar Felix and drew up before the hotel. Escipión, coming out of his office, smiled a welcome. Yes, he had a room with a balcony that overlooked the sea. How long was the *señor* thinking of staying?

"For a few days only." The Inspector sounded regretful.

"And your dog—" Like all hoteliers Escipión was wary of undisciplined pets.

"She is a lady in every sense of the word, except that she uses neither powder nor lipstick. She has stayed in many hotels, and she will neither sleep on the bed nor approach the other guests," he smiled, "until she has been introduced."

Escipión bent to pat the silky head. "Then I will have your case taken to your room. If you had wished to stay longer I should have had to tell you that we close next week. The season here is nearly over."

"You have other guests at the moment?"

"A small English tourist party and a *Señor* Warrack, a writer. The room I am giving you is separated from his by the linen room, so I do not think you will be disturbed by his typewriter." Escipión's brow creased in query as he watched the new guest follow the maid who had taken his suitcase.

A short time later the Inspector, having washed and unpacked, went out onto the balcony. Before the hotel stood a group of seven people. An alert, grey-haired woman seemed from her attitude and gestures to be trying, without success, to kindle enthusiasm in the other six. One by one they wandered off down the beach, except for a thin, neatly-busted brunette and an even thinner young man who walked, arms linked, past the hotel and disappeared into a cleft in the rocks, leading, as the Inspector knew from his map, to the inlet where the bodies had been found.

Miss Clegg had indeed been trying to interest at least one or two members of the 'Phoebus Abroad' party in another archaeological trip—but without much hope. The two married couples had merely looked dully at one another and, as if in wordless communication, shaken their heads. Beryl, taking Cyril by the arm, had declined firmly on his behalf as well as on her own.

"And how is your friend Millie?" Miss Clegg enquired. "She was not at lunch today, and I wondered whether she had had a recurrence of her stomach trouble. Is she lying down now?"

"You said it, auntie." Beryl winked at her escort. "She'll be on her back, like as not. Come on, Cyril me lad. Let's go to the little bay." She pulled him away proprietorially.

"Auntie." Miss Clegg repeated the word to herself with disgust. She would never become accustomed to modern familiarity, nor to uninhibited hints about a friend's sexual habits. It occurred to her, not for the first time, that she had been born a generation too late.

When the Inspector left the hotel he saw her leaning against a rock, a straw beach mat separating her poorly fleshed behind from the sand. Her knees supported a notebook of which the open pages were three-quarters filled with neatly pencilled paragraphs. She was scratching the tip of her nose with the blunt end of the pencil. As his passing momentarily occluded the sunshine she looked up.

"Good afternoon," he said in the tone of voice which allows the hearer the choice of merely acknowledging the greeting or of satisfying a desire for conversation.

"Good afternoon." She regarded him, then the dog, with interest. "I haven't seen you here before, have I? Is this your Bedlington?"

"Yes, this is Shadow. We've only just arrived at the hotel."

"Shadow." She repeated the name with approval, offered the back of her hand to the dog who sniffed at it, then rubbed her head against it in acceptance of friendship. "I'm staying at the hotel, too." Her stare was direct and penetrating. "You are obviously an intelligent person. Am I right in thinking that you have been to Ampurias?"

"The last time was some five years ago."

"Then you must go again. There's quite a lot of digging been done there since your visit and there are some interesting new finds. There were too many trippers there on Monday, and too many self-appointed guides giving people wrong information. I heard one man tell his friends that the Phoenicians were the first settlers there—and I'm afraid that in my usual meddlesome way I corrected him. He wasn't at all grateful."

The Inspector smiled. "Unless one is historically minded it's easy to confuse Phoenicia and Phocaea."

Her brisk nod was self-congratulatory. "I was certain you would know. If you're here for a few days and have nothing better to do we might have a chat. Well, I mustn't keep you from what you were going to do." Though her tone was dismissive, it seemed to the Inspector to derive not from a wish to get rid of him but from a fear of being thought a social burr. She put a hand into her bag and took out a pencil sharpener. In the brief moment that the contents of the bag became visible, the cover of a paperback caught his eye. The title of the book was *Candy*. She looked up, realizing that he had probably seen it and anticipating the smile and amused raising of the eyebrows which are so often the reaction to the discovery of reputed pornography in another person's possession. But the friendly expression on his face had not changed.

She gave a sudden chuckle. "Yes, *Candy*. It was a complete waste of my money and time—and now I'm stuck with it. I daren't throw it away in case someone sees me doing so. I was wondering about burying it in the sand, but if anyone saw me digging a deep hole they'd certainly come along to look. In any case, I haven't got a spade."

He held out his hand. "I'm going for a swim shortly. Let me give it a sea burial." He rolled the book in his towel.

As he went off a girl came out of the hotel, wearing the very tiniest of bikinis and carrying a beach mat. There was little that Nature could have done to improve her figure. Her short, blond curls framed a pretty, full-lipped face. She looks contented, he reflected—no, contented was an inadequate word; satisfied, like a puppy that has found within paw-reach the meat for a family of six. He found himself answering her smile while her eyes travelled him from head to toe. Walking on, he responded immediately to her assess-

55

ing gaze; his stride took on more spring; he drew in his already taut stomach. Vanity, he admonished himself: stupid, pleasurable vanity. Choosing a spot in the centre of the beach, he unrolled his towel and, tucking the copy of *Candy* into the band of his swimming shorts, waded into the water.

Shadow followed, paddling by his side. Twenty yards out, she gave a sharp bark, her signal that she had come her allotted distance. Returning to the beach, she shook herself vigorously, then stayed watching him with anxious eyes. Her vigilance would not cease until he returned.

In deep water the Inspector dived, then struck out into the bay. Soon he was level with the tip of Cap Rubí. Momentarily he considered swimming round the point to La Caleta; but he wished to be alone and, unless his surmise were wrong, the young couple he had seen would still be there and also desirous of privacy. Running through the list of names in the Magistrate's report, he identified the brunette as Beryl and the lad as Cyril. The almost Ingres blonde who had smiled at him was Millie. All three were surely the most unlikely of suspects.

Treading water, he ripped the back and front covers from the book and, tearing them up into small pieces, let them drift away. Page by page he took the letterpress apart, balled each sheet and let it go. Then, the knightly mission accomplished, he turned onto his back and floated. Few things, he had found, were so conducive to thought as the motion of a calm sea. Once again he began to consider some of the points in the Magistrate's report.

The pathologist's opinion was that all three had died within a short period; he had not been prepared to venture a close estimate of the times of death, but his general assessment did not conflict with Colin's statement that, when walking, he had observed a white boat with two passengers near Cap Rubí at approximately two o'clock, and that he had reached La Caleta forty or forty-five minutes later to find his aunt's dead body.

Examination of the bodies had disclosed some chafing of the skin at both back and front of Eldred's ankles. On the lobes of James's ears and on the inner part above the lobes were spots of extravasated blood. Clarice's forehead had been bruised while she was still alive, and a number of sea-urchin spines were lodged in the palm and fingers of her right hand. Other marks and scratches on the skin could be attributed to their immersion, or in Clarice's case part immersion, and to handling by the rescuers.

The boat had been partly filled with water. Experiment showed that, with two people aboard, it could have been overturned by injudicious or panic movement. The fuel tank of the outboard motor was completely empty.

From these facts and conjectures a number of theories could be evolved. The Pooles get into difficulties when the engine fails; perhaps one of them falls overboard. James, seeing what is happening, swims to their help. Alternatively, the Pooles, drifting into the inlet, find James struggling in the water—maybe he has had an attack of cramp or has swum beyond his strength—and attempt to rescue him. The boat tips over as they try to pull him out, and all three are in the sea. As the boat drifts away from them, Eldred calls to Clarice to make for the nearest point of land and, swimming on his back, grips James by the head and endeavours to bring him ashore. James slips or struggles from Eldred's grasp, snatches at his ankles and drags him to their joint death. Clarice reaches the rocks, scrabbles at the sea-urchin covered surface and, completely exhausted, falls and drowns.

These were possibilities; there were almost certainly others. No one had seen what occurred—or, rather, no one had offered any information. James's sun umbrella had been planted in the sand near the cleft that led to Cala Felix and in the shelter of the steep incline of Cap Rubí; it was not visible from Cala Felix—in fact it could be seen only from the sea, from a short stretch of the road and from some not too distant heights. Colin had viewed it from these heights, and one point that he had mentioned to the *Teniente* had interested the latter and the Magistrate. For Colin had noticed, or said that he had noticed, two towels beside the umbrella. Thersie, on the other hand, was sure that when she arrived there was only one towel and that Clarice was lying face downwards on it while Colin tried to revive her. Colin was unable to recall the colour of the second towel, but thought it might have been multi-coloured—as, of course, were most of the beach towels in everyday use. The question, then, was: Had there been a second towel? If not, why should Colin have declared that there had been? The answer, or rather an answer, was that Colin had wished it to be thought that James had a companion on the beach—and that this companion had not been Colin.

The Inspector hand-paddled gently. Colin was, so far as he himself knew, a wealthy and childless woman's sole nephew. But a sole nephew is not necessarily an heir; and, even if he is an heir, a financial motive does not necessarily create a murderer. Nor need murder spring from motive; it was very often an act of impulse—or of idiocy.

Superficially, Colin had an alibi—but one so far unsupported by any witnesses. As for the others—Basil had told the *Teniente* that he had been meeting Antonia at Flassá; Miss Clegg and the other members of the tour party, with the exception of Millie, had been at Ampurias; Bill Eddow out in the launch; Escipión and Gregory in the hotel; Juan, Carmen and Enrique in the Bar Felix. Their stories must be checked again as fully as possible and further inquiry made about the possibility of any other visitor to the neighbourhood. There remained the Strongitharm brothers who, according to Carmen, had driven off south at about half past two—after the presumed time of the drownings—and had told her that they would return today.

The Inspector turned onto his face and struck out for the shore. He was drying himself, Shadow relieved and contented at his feet, when a friendly voice said, "Hullo," and he turned to see the man who had preceded him at the petrol station.

"You staying here?" asked Basil. "No, that's a stupid question. I saw you take your suitcase into the hotel."

"I could have been a commercial traveller making a call." The Inspector smiled. "Yes, I'll probably be staying here for

58

a few days. It seems so tranquil, a place where nothing could ever happen to disturb one's peace."

"Yes, it looks peaceful." There was a certain dryness in Basil's voice. "I hope you'll find it so." He liked the look of this man who was so unobtrusively sizing him up. Well, I'm sizing him up too, he reflected, noting the ring on the right hand, recalling that the grey car had carried a Barcelona registration plate, and taking in the clearly well-bred English dog which in its turn was eying him appraisingly.

"Bas-il." Antonia's voice called. "The gas ring's gone out, and I think the cylinder's empty. I can't even lift the spare one." A slight figure, boy-like in blue jeans and loose blue shirt, beckoned from a bungalow doorway. Sunshine burnished the cropped chestnut hair and lit the contours of a charming urchin face.

"I must go and give Antonia a hand." Basil gave an answering wave. "Come in and see us when you feel like a chat. If we're not on the beach, nine times out of ten you'll find us at home."

Watching Basil lope easily away, the Inspector decided that further concealment of his identity would serve no purpose. He felt pretty sure that Escipión had guessed it. There could be little doubt that every Spaniard here was aware of the tenor of the Magistrate's report. The bush telegraph had no such limitations as the national telephone service. Soon, if it had not already done so, the news would reach the Spanish-speaking visitors and, through them, those whose knowledge of the language was slight or non-existent. Draping his towel round his neck, he made his way to the hotel, Shadow padding at his heels.

In the foyer Miss Clegg was talking to a fair-haired man whose nebulously good-looking face wore an unconvincing expression of apology. "No, you don't have to apologize, Mr Eddow," she was saying without unkindness. "I don't need an escort. All I ask is that you arrange for a car on Saturday to take me and anyone else who may wish to go to Ampurias and Perelada."

"I really think I should stay here," Bill replied with relief.

"I know that at least four of the party won't want to go, and I think I should remain with the majority."

Miss Clegg's gentle snort of amusement was masterly. "Of course you shall stay with them." She sighed. "I suppose history's out of fashion nowadays—but, good heavens, we're surrounded by it here. Even this hotel's called after the Emperor Hadrian, and the manager's name is Scipio. The whole region *reeks* of the past."

"*Le mot juste,*" said Gregory's voice from behind her. "The drains run into the bay, the river at Gerona's like an open sewer, the rubbish tip at the back of the hotel stinks of God knows what. You have a gift for the appropriate phrase, Miss Clegg. By the way, did I hear you trying to organize another archaeological orgy later in the week?"

"I intend to see Ampurias again," she answered composedly. "A visit there might help to widen your regrettably narrow horizon."

Gregory grinned. "My field of ignorance is extensive—and I'm happy that it should increase every day. The less I know, the less I'm likely to be worried. Ignorance *is* bliss, you know. The man who knows too much is never contented."

"Rubbish!" she exploded. "No one can ever know enough. Do you want a world of people who are interested only in themselves, the weather and what they're going to stuff into their stomachs—like a lot of cows at pasture?"

"I'd let a bull into the field occasionally to keep them aware of the facts of life."

"The facts of life," she repeated contemptuously. "I suppose that by that revolting cliché you mean sex. Heavens, man, there are a myriad other facts of life. Sex is just a function that we share with the louse and the lamprey. It's productive only in the sense that it enables a species to perpetuate itself."

"You're trying to provoke me into an argument which I haven't got the brains to sustain." Gregory lowered his eyes in mock humility. "If I were to say that sex has inspired some of the world's finest art, you'd tell me that the actual inspiration arose from sheer appreciation of beauty, whether living or inanimate. So what I will say is that for the larger part of humanity sex is the fact—the topic, if you prefer—that never loses its interest. And, if one is trying to make a living by writing fiction, as I hope to do, a dollop or two of sex can make the difference between selling a couple of thousand copies and fifty or a hundred thousand." He gave an amused shrug. "One of the unarguable facts of life is that at least half the reading public are sexual Walter Mittys. They like to read about what they haven't and never will experience. They're the target I'm aiming at—and I seem to have been lucky enough to score an inner with my opening shot."

"And you're satisfied with the result?" It was a rhetorical question. His tone of voice had already supplied the answer; but she was curious to know whether he would pretend to a modicum of modesty.

"Eminently." He chuckled. "Do I detect a note of disapproval? Aren't you passing judgment before you've heard the case? Wouldn't it be fairer to read the book first?"

"Would you like me to read it?" she asked.

He looked at her, a crooked smile on his lips, then shook his head. "Frankly, no. I'm going for a swim now. I'll be in the bar at seven. Join me and I'll stand you a gin and tonic."

"Make it a double and I'll be there," Miss Clegg said promptly. She thoroughly enjoyed the drinks which she could not afford in England and, after the closed and often bitchy circle in the staff room at her school, found considerable pleasure in crossing verbal swords with Gregory.

After showering and donning a clean shirt and slacks, the Inspector left the hotel and stood contemplatively on the steps. Outside one of the renting bungalows a large and powerful estate car had now arrived. The rear door was open, and the roof rack partly unloaded. From the bungalow two muscular figures emerged, bare to the waist. As with many red-haired people, long exposure to the sun had turned their skins an almost fluorescent pink.

"Let's give it a rest now," the one with the slightly

crooked nose was saying as the Inspector came within earshot. "The stuff's safe enough where it is. No one's going to knock it off while we're around."

The Inspector glanced into the open back of the car. Black foam diving suits, masks, oxygen bottles, harness, fins and other pieces of underwater equipment covered the floor. Among them a baby's blue plastic rattle struck a note of incongruity. Smilingly the Inspector commented, "You've got some fine equipment there."

"Best there is, ain't it, Jack?" the crooked-nosed one said, glancing at his brother for unnecessary confirmation. "It don't do to have cheap stuff. Fifty quid in the bank's not much use if you've got air bubbles in the brain-box." He eyed the Inspector from head to foot. "Do any underwater stuff yourself?"

"Just a little." To the hearers it was clearly an understatement.

"Got your gear with you?"

"Not this time, I'm afraid."

"Can you handle a boat?"

"So long as there isn't a back-seat driver."

Perce chuckled at the response. "Sounds as if we might get along together. Tell you what. Our pal what had his boat nearby's gone off home. If you've a fancy to come out with us, Juan'd let us have the launch. I reckon one of our suits'd fit you nice and snug—we c'd see. If you're around tomorrow, give us the word. Right now we're flaked out. Been down the coast—taking some pictures."

"Didn't fancy it much there, so we come back quick." Jack cleared his throat. "What about that beer we was talking about, Perce?"

"Some in the fridge. Come and have a drop with us, and your dog can have a sup of water or whatever she fancies. Jack and me's had enough of our own company—and we needs a rub-down and something to wash the dust off our tongues." Hand on the Inspector's shoulder, he gave him a friendly shove towards the bungalow. "We'll be staying on another week."

"Might get another few hundred feet of film if the weather stays like it is. I'll take the first shower, Perce, and you give our chum hero a glass of wallop." Jack paused interrogatively. "Don't think we've got your name."

"Salvador Borges." To these just-arrived men who could only be the Strongitharms he would not disclose his identity immediately.

"Spaniard, are you?" Jack was surprised. "Wouldn't have guessed it. On holiday?"

"Just a few days away from Barcelona."

As Jack went off to the bathroom, Perce, filling glasses from a bottle of beer, remarked, "There was some likely folk here when we went off. Seen any of 'em?"

"Some." The violet eyes rested on Perce's. "Three of them were drowned on Monday."

"Drowned?" The bottle thumped on the table. "Who was they?" He listened to the names. "Cor, strike me pink. Poor buggers. What happened?"

The Inspector told him briefly.

"Must have been after we went off, I s'pose?"

"What time was that?"

"Around half two."

"It happened in the next bay." The Inspector gestured southwards.

"But I saw them Pooles in the little boat earlier on—must have been a bit after ten. Half a mile out, they was and making southwest. There was only the two of them."

"Mr Rowley was spending the day at La Caleta."

"On his tod." Seeing the Inspector's look of incomprehension, Perce added, "There weren't no one with him?"

"It seems not," the Inspector replied as Jack returned carrying another bottle. He listened while Perce passed on the news. Jack filled his glass in silence. He appeared as interested in avoiding a head on the beer as in what his brother was saying.

"Poor bastards," he commented. "Pity we wasn't here at the time. We might've been able to save the lot. Had a shot at it anyway."

"I think you were here." The Inspector shook his head as Perce pushed the bottle towards him. "At least I gather your car was outside the bungalow."

"If the car was here, we was," Perce said definitely. "We got back from diving just on one, and we was off, as I said, about half two. We packed the car up, came in for a bite, locked up and stopped to leave the key with Carmen. Maybe we was indoors when those folk got into trouble, 'cos we never heard a thing."

"We had the radio on for the news. 'Spect you remember, Perce, there'd been a down-tools in one of the car factories 'cos the canteen'd been using powdered milk. Some of the blokes cut up rough, and one of the waitresses poured his cupful over his head. If we hadn't had it on, we might have heard if anyone shouted for help, which I 'spect they did." He stretched out a hand to his glass. "Suppose there's been an inquest or something of the sort?"

The Inspector did not answer the question directly. "They were buried this morning." After a pause, he asked, "Did you see anyone around during the hour and a half before you left?"

"Only Carmen. There wasn't no one on the beach, was there, Jack?"

"Didn't see anyone."

The second bottle was empty when the Inspector left. "Seems a decent sort of bloke," Jack observed when they were alone. "Listens. Don't say much." After a moment he added, "If he's on holiday, I'm the Beatles' Aunt Fanny."

"Will you have supper with me tonight?" asked Colin. "There's an awful lot of food in the fridge."

"I'd love to." Thersie smiled inwardly at the manner of the invitation; but she knew that he liked her company as much as she liked his. Later, when she was mixing a salad in the Pooles' kitchen, she asked how long he would be staying at Cala Felix.

"I don't know. The *Teniente* said I must wait until permission to leave is given. I suppose there'll be various formalities to be completed and papers to be signed." He was unaware, as was Thersie, of the Inspector's arrival and of the rumours that had preceded it. "And I'll have to close up the bungalow and ask Carmen to look after it until we know what's to be done about it." He hesitated slightly before inquiring casually, "You'll be here, won't you?"

"Until my parents leave at the end of the month." She put the salad bowl on the table. "Everything's ready. Let's sit down, and you can go on telling me about the things you've done since you came down from Cambridge."

"There's nothing more to tell. I've never done anything really exciting."

"Then tell me the dull things." She looked at the square-chinned face bent over the plate of cold meats and caught his eye. Suddenly they both laughed.

6

Wednesday evening, 13ᵗʰ September

THE BAR FELIX was empty except for Enrique who roused himself from a frowning study of the current football coupon to pour out the requested glass of mineral water and to fetch, without being asked, a bowl of water at which Shadow lapped gratefully.

The Inspector took a stool at the corner where the curve of the bar met the wall. Idly he picked up a book that had been left there and, turning it over, read the title, *No End of a World*. A neat double meaning, he said to himself, as he opened it to glance at the blurb on the flap of the dust-jacket.

"Gregory Warrack," he read, "is already well known as a script-writer. In this, his first novel, he establishes himself among the master writers of suspense stories . . . Barry Crisp, a clerk in a toy factory, suddenly finds himself caught up in a plot to kidnap a diplomat. Himself kidnapped, he is pitched into a terrifying world of treachery, sadism, lust, torture . . ." The Inspector's eye travelled downwards. In a heavily framed box Gothic capitals spelled out, "WARNING. THIS IS NOT A BOOK FOR PRUDES."

The back flap carried a photograph of the author. It was an admirable portrait study. The Inspector could almost hear the lazy tones of the man who a short time ago had been quizzing Miss Clegg in the hotel foyer.

"Looking at Greg's book?" asked a purring voice. "I'll

tell you, it fair gave me the willies. Hardly got a wink of sleep last night. As poor old James said, he can lay it on all right." A small, finely modelled hand brushed the Inspector's wrist as a finger touched the picture. "Just like him, the spitting image." She picked up the book. "Promised I wouldn't let anyone else see it. I put it here so's not to forget to give it back when he comes in."

The Inspector took in the pretty, vivid face crowned by a mop of dark curls. Behind the fresh make-up, the long eyelashes, the eye shadow and the beauty spot on the cheek bubbled a personality that brought the bar to bounding life. "I saw him in the hotel a short time ago," he mentioned.

"I heard you'd come." The tiniest of frowns marked her forehead. "Is it right that you're a policeman?"

He smiled assent.

"Well!" She met his gentle gaze and put her elbows on the counter. "When the word went round that it wasn't an accident, all them three drowning like that, I thought we'd have cops all over the place waving guns and giving us all the third degree." She paused, then asked suspiciously, "Are there a lot more of you coming?"

He shook his head. "You're *Señora* Carosco?"

"Call me Carmen." Her eyelids fluttered in mock flirtation. "Everyone does. 'Smatter of fact, my real name's Gladys, but you couldn't run a bar here with a name like that, so I took to Carmen 'cos it's got a bit of romance about it. 'Sides, now that I've picked up the lingo, a lot of 'em tell me what good English I speak—gives me a good laugh as I come from Birmingham—and they bring their pals along and we have a bit of fun. Juan gets a bit uppity when they start trying to get fresh, but," she held up a sturdy arm, "I can look after myself all right, and it's good for trade. If a chap like poor old Eldred wanted a kiss and a peek down your dress it didn't do anyone any harm." She glanced up as the door opened. "Hello, Greg. You look as if you could do with a stiff one. The usual?" She beckoned to Enrique as he came in from the kitchen, then looked questioningly at the Inspector, uncertain whether she should introduce them.

He introduced himself.

"A policeman," commented Gregory as he shook hands. "On leave?" He snapped his fingers at Shadow who lay curled up between counter and stool.

The Inspector shook his head. "I fear not."

Gregory looked at him sharply. "But in plain clothes. I assume that the local people now have the assistance of someone from whatever is your equivalent to Scotland Yard. So things weren't what they seemed? Or am I wrong in guessing that you are here in connection with the three drownings?"

"Things may well be as they seemed." The tone was mild. "But naturally any relatives and the police would like to know what happened and why."

"There's one thing I can tell you," Carmen said after a short silence. "Clarice and Eldred went off in the boat before Juan had filled her up. He saw them going off and shouted, but I s'pose they didn't hear him. When Bill took the launch out Juan gave him a can of petrol to hand over if he saw them."

"Well, that's one query answered," Gregory commented. "I don't know what ideas anyone else has, but my guess would be that they got into a panic when the engine stopped and the boat started drifting onto the rocks. They seemed a pretty unhandy pair, and I'd think they managed to upset the boat and that James went to their help. Probably he arrived too late and was too exhausted to get back. He shouldn't have tried in his state of health. You know he damned nearly died a few months ago." He sipped at his drink. "We were old friends, James and I. We worked together on the script of *Lark in the Air* and got to know one another pretty well. He was one of the best in the business— fantastic imagination and wonderful dialogue. I'd an idea for a film, and we thought we might get together on it." He sighed. "And the next day he was dead."

"You say he had been very ill. Was he at all depressed?"

"Far from it. He was working on something and had nearly finished it." Gregory met the Inspector's eye. "If you've got any idea of suicide, and that the Pooles were trying to prevent it, you can put that right out of your mind. James wasn't the sort who'd think of taking his own life—and who in the world would dream of drowning himself when half a bottle of aspirin will send you to sleep for good? Hullo, Miss Clegg. This is—Oh, you know the Inspector, do you?"

"Yes, we met this afternoon on the beach." Momentarily she seemed taken aback, then she chuckled. "If I'd known you were a policeman I wouldn't have dreamed of asking you to perform that small service for me."

"I was a volunteer," he said, "and delighted to be able to do something so simple."

"Let's hope you clear up this drowning business as easily," observed Gregory. "If there's anything I can do to help, just ask. I'm sure the same goes for all of us." He gave a wry half-laugh. "Or shouldn't I assume that none of us is under suspicion?"

"Not yet perhaps," the Inspector answered blandly. "I shall, however, very much appreciate your help. You can, for instance, give me some idea of what sort of people the Pooles and James Rowley were. Some people carry in themselves the seeds of accident—impatience, over-confidence, conceit —" He let the sentence die away.

"I've told you what I think about James," said Gregory. "He was level-headed and modest. If he had any faults I don't know of them. He'd a charming wife, but she died some years ago. Having no children was his greatest regret. He wasn't exactly a social chap, but everyone liked him." He glanced interrogatively at Miss Clegg.

"I talked to him once on Sunday," she said shortly, picking up her gin and tonic. "I didn't have much conversation with the Pooles. I found him self-opinionated and rather a busybody. Odd," she went on thoughtfully, "that neither of them had made a will until the night before they died."

The Inspector's raised head was an invitation to continue.

"I suppose they were the sort of people who don't like to think about dying. But someone they knew had died recently without making a will, and there was going to be some legal nonsense about the division of the estate. Eldred talked about it ad nauseam here in the bar, produced a couple of stationers' will forms which Clarice and he had completed, and asked Carmen and me to witness their signatures. I'm afraid I couldn't help reading his will," she confessed with a slight heightening of colour. "I'm an inquisitive old besom. I don't recall the exact words, but his will left everything he possessed to Clarice. I think there was a second Christian name, but—"

"Huntingdon," Carmen supplied the name without a pause. "Of course I read his will too—both of them. And she wrote the same—I mean, leaving it all to him. Funny wasn't it, them not thinking of anyone else? I bet they were both worth a packet. I wonder," she went on wistfully, "who gets it now."

"Probably their next of kin," said Gregory. "By the way, has anyone seen Colin? Oughtn't we to find him and get him along? Cheer him up as much as we can."

"I wouldn't poke my nose in where I wasn't wanted," Carmen told him. "I saw Thersie going into his place a while back. She's a good kid, and she's on her own. I'd leave them be. If they want company they know where to find it."

Half an hour later they were again reminiscing about those who had so unexpectedly died. Perce and Jack had finished unloading their car and were leaning against the counter.

"'Member what Clarice said about that robbery at her bank in Downchester," Carmen was saying as Antonia and Basil came in. "Poor thing. She'll never tell the police about what she saw."

"What did she see?" Antonia enquired.

"A man coming out of the side door. She'd gone to the bank at half past nine, found it closed and got tired of wait-ing. I think she said something about the front of the bank being cleaned. It was all in last week's papers, but I 'spect they've been thrown away."

"Perhaps I could help." Miss Clegg took over with the

70

firmness of a teacher whose life has been one long struggle against recalcitrant memories. Concisely she recalled what Clarice had told them. "As for the man she saw leaving by the door in the side street, he was wearing white overalls and a cap, and he had steel-framed spectacles."

"He wasn't carrying any loot as far as I remember," Gregory offered.

"He was taking off rubber gloves," Miss Clegg went on, "and she noticed a ring on his little finger. She didn't say what sort, but, unless he was a foreigner, it was probably a signet ring. My brother has one, a lapis lazuli incised with a cleg."

"With a *what*?" queried Carmen.

"A cleg. A kind of insect. Old Norse word. Our family crest." Rapidly changing the subject before she was compelled by a further question to disclose that a cleg was that objectionable and unclean creature, a horse-fly, she went on, "But I wouldn't expect a workman to be wearing one."

"Perhaps he, too, has a family crest." Gregory grinned wickedly. "But, whatever it was, I agree with what was said at the time. The police should be told. It might help to identify one of the robbers. Of course," he turned to the Inspector, "I suppose the police have now been told. Can we leave it to you to pass on anything you think may be of importance? Now, what about another drink, Miss Clegg—all of you? Plenty of time before dinner." He signed to Enrique.

The Inspector declined and, taking Carmen aside, asked, "Can you remember who was here when the Pooles were talking about their wills and having their signatures witnessed?"

"Just Miss Clegg and me and Beryl with her boyfriend—oh, and Enrique was in and out."

"And when Mrs Poole was speaking about the bank robbery?"

"You've got me there. Let's think." Carmen searched her recollection. "Enrique for sure, and Miss Clegg and me; and Thersie because she'd had her grub with us; Basil and Gregory, and Perce and Jack. Oh, James was there; it was the last time I saw him. And Juan must have come in because Eldred asked him about having the boat in the morning. I think that's the lot. Bill, the chap in charge of the tour came in as Clarice and Eldred were going. He must have come across them somewhere before, as he seemed surprised and pleased to see Clarice—though I got a feeling that Eldred wasn't so pleased."

"By something one of them said?"

"I didn't hear anything, but when Bill held out his hand Eldred didn't seem to see it. Clarice had already shaken hands. She was a nice little thing, Clarice. Come to that, she was a bit too nice or she'd have given Eldred a clip over the earhole sometimes. He was a messer-about, had those wandering hands, if you know what I mean, and, as for kissing—well, he had a kiss like a dish-cloth that's not been wrung out." She passed a remembering hand over her lips. "I'm sorry he's dead, of course, but I can't say that I'll miss him. He wasn't my cup of tea—and, to tell you the truth, I don't think he was anyone else's."

What sadder epitaph could any man have? the Inspector reflected. "And now," he said, "do you mind telling me what you were doing between half past one and half past two on Monday?"

"Of course I don't. It's your job to ask questions, isn't it? I gave the kids their meal at half past one. Had my own, too, and then put them upstairs to lie down for an hour. That's a regular thing. Then I was in the kitchen while Enrique had his food. I was messing about there when Perce and Jack looked in to say they were popping down south for a couple of days. They had a glass of beer, gave me their key to look after and were off just after half past two."

"Did Juan have lunch with you and the children?"

"He had it later when he came in from the back," she said as if the matter required no further explanation.

"At what time, Carmen?"

"A minute or two after Perce and Jack went off."

"He told the *Teniente* that he was here from one o'clock onwards—and you confirmed it."

"Of course I did. If he said he was, he was." She leaned forward earnestly. "Look, Juan didn't need to lie—and I've have known if he wasn't telling the truth. If you think he had anything against those three you've got the wrong idea. He liked James a lot, and he'd a soft spot for Clarice. He didn't think too much of Eldred, and he didn't fancy the way Eldred always wanted to get his hands on me." She gave a little shrug. "We had a bit of a spat Sunday night because Eldred gave me a mingy bottle of scent. 'Smatter of fact, Juan chucked it out of the window. Monday morning he wasn't speaking unless he had to. He was up late and, when he'd seen Bill off in the launch, he went out to the shed and tinkered about with something. He does that when he's got a mood on. I heard him hammering away once or twice. I kept his lunch hot for him, and when he came in he'd found his temper again. Mind you, he didn't say he was sorry or anything like that, but when he gave me a slap on the bottom I knew everything was all right again." She raised her head, listening. "That's one of the kids calling. See you later." She fluttered her eyelashes and was off.

The Inspector made an unobtrusive departure. There was still some time before dinner would be served at the hotel, although for the sake of the English guests meal times had been advanced half an hour. He turned right along the road to the owner-occupied bungalows. The first one, he knew, was empty. In the second, Basil's, lights had been left burning. The next three were dark and shuttered. Strolling along under the darkening sky, he thought of the wills which the Pooles had made. Unless they had been sent for safe-keeping to England—but when could they have been sent?—they must, or should be in the bungalow. Surely Colin would have looked for them. But could they have any bearing on his own inquiries? No one except the Pooles and the two witnesses could have known their contents—unless one of the four had spoken of them, or unless someone had found the wills and read them before the Pooles died.

Rounding the shoreward side of the banjo, he approached the Pooles' bungalow. There were lights in the sitting-room, and on the terrace where three people sat talking. Two of them would be Colin and Thersie. Who was the third, the man whose back was turned to the terrace rail? In the still air voices came distinctly. These three, too, were speaking of wills. Colin asked a question, and the other man was replying. The Inspector stopped to listen. Shortly, signing to Shadow to stay where she was, he moved forward.

"I'd like to spend a year or two in America," said Colin as he helped Thersie to clear the table. "There's so much more scope and money there for research of every kind—grants, and private finance from millionaires who have hearts of gold and good tax advisers. In any case, I don't think one can really appreciate one's own country until one's seen how other people live."

Thersie nodded agreement. "I'd like to see more of the world, too. But I've got to earn a living, and I don't know much about anything except cars."

"You drive beautifully, Thersie. I feel safe with you."

And you're one of the few men I've driven about in Spain, she reflected, who hasn't made me wonder whether I'll have to grope for the spanner under the driving-seat. It was in companionable silence that they took glasses of Anis onto the terrace. They had scarcely sat down when a man came up the steps, hovered indecisively and then advanced. "My name is Bill Eddow," he said to Colin. "Could I talk to you for a moment?"

"Do sit down." Pulling up a chair, Colin introduced Thersie. "I'm sure I've heard the name Eddow before."

"Quite possibly." Bill smiled nervously. "I'm some sort of relation—no, connection, I suppose. Eldred was my half-brother. We had the same mother, and I was the only child of her second marriage."

"You're Eldred's half-brother." Colin caught Thersie's astonished eye. "But why—?"

"Why didn't I say so when he and Clarice were drowned?" He gave a self-deprecatory shrug. "Because there wasn't really anything for me to do. You were seeing to things, and there wasn't any purpose in my butting in. Besides, I scarcely knew them. I don't suppose I'd seen them more than three times in my life, and Eldred had made it clear that he didn't want to have anything to do with me."

"But why? Had you quarrelled or done something to offend him?"

Bill shook his head. "I'd done nothing wrong except be my mother's son. She left Eldred's father because he was a complete bastard. After the divorce, Eldred said he never wanted to see her again, and he didn't. I wrote to him when she died, but he didn't even reply. Then, a few years ago when I'd just come out of hospital and couldn't find a job, I went to see him. He treated me as if I were some sort of tout, refused to help me in any way and said I need never expect anything from him. Clarice helped me without his knowledge and said she'd always do so if I were in difficulties." He looked down, avoiding Colin's eye. "I suppose I should have said something when they died, but what good would it have done? There was nothing I could have told anyone."

"Then why are you telling us now?" A sudden certainty about the reason made Colin's voice colder than he intended.

"Well—" Bill shifted awkwardly in his chair. Intent on what he was about to say, none of them heard the quiet footsteps on the road. "Well, Beryl said something today about them both having made wills the night before they were drowned—and I thought perhaps you'd seen the wills and could tell me if I'd been left anything."

The silence was broken by the sound of someone approaching. In a moment the Inspector reached the terrace. "Good evening," he said, "I am sorry to disturb you." He looked round the three upraised faces. "I fear that I overheard what you were saying, Mr Eddow. Why should you expect your name to appear in either will?"

He listened without change of expression to the halting explanation. "I see," was all he said before turning to Colin and asking, "Have you read the wills?"

"No, I didn't even know that they were here, or that

they'd just been made. I assumed they'd be in England."
Colin rose and, inviting the Inspector to sit down, found
himself another chair. "You're sure that they were actually
made *here*?"

"Quite sure." The Inspector remained standing. "I think
we had better look for them now."

Colin made no move. Frowning, he asked, "But why
should you wish to see them?"

"You will no doubt wish to see them yourself. And you
will agree that, if they are here, they should be found. Mr
Eddow knows who I am, but I see you do not." He introduced himself. "I have been asked to complete the inquiry
into the deaths of your aunt and uncle. It will be incomplete
until we know what has happened to their wills." He took in
the expression on Colin's face. "I can see that you wish to
ask me some questions. Let us look for the wills—and then I
will do my best to answer you."

Colin led the way into the sitting-room. There was indeed
a question in his mind, but it could be deferred until this
courteously determined policeman had satisfied his curiosity.
He waited for him to speak.

"Will you take the drawers on this side of the desk, Mr
Dennison, and I will take the drawers on the other side and
the centre drawer. Perhaps, Miss Sallis, you would be good
enough to look in the bedroom." He said nothing to Bill
who, after fidgeting around, sat down heavily.

Taking out the top drawer, Colin knelt on the floor and
began to examine the overflowing contents. This side of the
desk, he realized, must have been his aunt's. Letters, bills,
used envelopes, emery boards, a fountain pen without a cap,
samples of furnishing materials, a colour-card of paints, a
packet of needles—it was a collection so typical of his un-
methodical aunt that it brought her vividly into his mind.
When at last he had looked into every envelope and
crammed everything back into the drawer, he noted that the
papers which the Inspector was handling were tied or clipped
together in a fashion that showed his uncle's meticulous
hand. Opening the next drawer, he found some sheets of die-

76

stamped writing-paper and two small empty boxes which, judging by the silver bells on the labels, had clearly once contained slices of wedding cake. The third drawer held only an empty chocolate box, and the bottom drawer nothing but a little dust. He was pushing it back as the Inspector closed the centre drawer from which he had taken a long-barrelled key.

"This looks like a safe key." The Inspector glanced round the half-dozen hunting prints on the wall and, walking over to one, lifted it, disclosing a square steel door. The key turned smoothly in the lock. From the safe he took a rubber-banded packet of Bank of England notes, a booklet of travellers' cheques, a folded sheet of paper and a passport, which he opened. "Your uncle's passport," he said, "and this is a will form. Perhaps you would like to read it, Mr Dennison."

"He left everything to my aunt," Colin said after a moment. Out of the corner of his eye he saw Bill shrug as if this was what he had expected.

"I can't find anything that looks like a will." Thersie returned as Colin was speaking. "It's not in any of the drawers or the three handbags there, and I've looked in the pockets of her clothes." She hesitated before continuing, "I heard her say on Sunday night that she wanted to add something to her will." She explained how she had unintentionally eavesdropped, and repeated Eldred's curt reply of "Then you can add a codicil tomorrow."

"Did you happen to hear what the codicil was about?" the Inspector inquired.

"She wanted to leave someone ten thousand pounds." Thersie met the soft, violet eyes so directly that he knew she could tell him more. There was little doubt in his mind that she had not told him because to do so might disappoint somebody if the codicil had not been added.

"It was to Mr Dennison?" he asked, and after a long moment she nodded.

"Dear Aunt Clarice," Colin said quietly. "If she added the codicil, God bless her. If she didn't —well, she meant to."

His voice was sad as he went on, "Why didn't I reach her in time? A little sooner and we might have been able to revive her."

"Or you might have been able to tell us what happened." The inspector paused. "Do you need me to tell you why I am here?"

For a short time there was no sound in the room except for the gentle background murmur of the sea. "Not now," Colin answered at last. "You are not satisfied that the deaths were accidental. You may even suspect someone here of being responsible for them."

"I suspect no one. If it was a tragic accident, then let us try and prove it. You may think you know nothing, but anything you recall might well help to establish the facts. You, Colin," his tone and the use of the Christian name brought a note of disarming friendliness and sympathy into the conversation, "you told the *Teniente* that, when you first came in sight of La Caleta, you saw two towels by the sun umbrella. You are quite sure there were two?"

"Good Lord, I'd entirely forgotten." Colin thought briefly. "Yes, I'm quite certain."

"And you, Thersie, are you sure that, when you arrived, there was only one?"

"Quite sure—only the towel on which Colin had put his aunt."

"Can you remember the colour of the towels?" he asked Colin.

"I doubt whether I could distinguish them from where I was at the time. I must have been several hundred yards away—I mean in the direct line of sight; it was very much further on foot. The towel on which I put my aunt was a black and green check."

"Could you possibly have mistaken Mr Rowley's shirt or his beachbag for a second towel?"

"I didn't notice them until later. They were both lying behind the air mattress in the shade of the umbrella."

"I understand that you arrived at La Caleta at about twenty to three?"

"Yes, or a little later. I left Torroella de Montgrí at nine o'clock, and I'd been walking for some five hours when I saw the white dinghy coming up the coast. Perhaps five minutes afterwards I came in sight of the cove and saw somebody bathing. Then I went on to a clump of pinetrees, sat down for say a quarter of an hour and ate a roll and some fruit. When I started off again up the next rise I'd been walking for a few minutes when the cove came into sight again and I saw the boat floating empty and apparently waterlogged, and not a sign of the people who'd been in it or of the bather. It looked to me as if there might have been some sort of accident, so I went down as fast as I could. And then, when I got there—I found my aunt's body and carried her to the beach. I was trying to revive her when Thersie came along and took over from me."

He sounds as if he were telling the truth, the Inspector said to himself. His eyes have remained steady, and he has spoken simply, without any embellishments. "Did you meet anyone on your way from Torroella?" he asked.

"Quite a few people—and I passed men working in the fields and one or two sites where builders were at work."

"But no one you knew?"

"No one." Colin smiled. "After all, I'd never been here before."

"And you, Thersie, were returning from San Feliu?"

"Yes. I stopped on the way for coffee and a sandwich. It was about three o'clock, perhaps five to, when I saw the empty boat—and then Colin trying desperately to revive someone."

"Did you see anybody else nearby?"

"No one at all."

The Inspector half turned his head. "And now, Mr Eddow, what can you tell me?"

Bill, who had been sitting, nervously pensive since he entered, started almost violently. "Sorry, I was dreaming. No one except Miss Clegg ever calls me anything but Bill. Me—well, I skipped the tour on Monday because, frankly, Ampurias bores me and in any case Miss Clegg would make a very much better guide. I borrowed Juan's launch, went for a spin, fished a bit without any success, put in at—at Calella, sat for a time at a café, then went down to the beach for a swim. I lay in the sun for a while and got back here about half past three. I was having a word with Escipión when the Civil Guard came along to collect a diving party."

"You never saw the Pooles' boat?"

"No. I looked for it. Juan said they hadn't much fuel and gave me a can to hand over if I saw them. But they must have put in somewhere where they couldn't be seen from the sea."

"Did you meet or talk to anyone you knew at Calella?"

Bill shook his head. "I expect, if you ask around, you'll find some people who saw me." He was gaining confidence as he talked. "I'm quite well known in these parts, though," he gave a wry grin, "not perhaps as someone of the highest character."

"You've been here for some time, then?"

"Not at Cala Felix. I've couriered for 'Phoebus Abroad' since June, but the previous parties stayed at Llafranch."

"Did you know that the Pooles had a bungalow here?"

"No, I didn't. I hadn't seen either of them for a long time."

"Surely someone here must have mentioned their name?"

"Carmen, or it may have been Juan, did speak of some Pooles, but it never occurred to me that they might be Clarice and Eldred. Poole's a pretty common name, you know."

The Inspector made no comment. After a pause he said, "Thank you—Bill. If you should remember anything you haven't told me you can let me know later."

"Yes, of course." Bill accepted the implied dismissal with alacrity. "I'll be off now to keep an eye on my party." With a muttered "Good night" he was gone.

Asking Colin for his uncle's will, the Inspector put it into his pocket. Was there any reason why Colin and Thersie should not continue the search for Clarice's will? He thought not. Declining her offer of a drink or a cup of coffee, he

80

asked them to go on looking. "I would also like to have her passport," he added.

Passing Basil's bungalow, he heard Antonia's voice through the open sitting-room window. "Did you remember to repay Carmen the ten pesetas she tipped the telegram boy on Saturday?"

"No, I forgot again. Remind me tomorrow." Basil's reply came from another part of the bungalow. "My god, Antonia, your clothes are everywhere. You're the untidiest wench I've ever shared a room with."

"I'm the last one you'll ever share with," she called back gaily. "You'll get used to it."

" 'Were I laid in Greeland's coast,' " Basil sang in a rusty baritone, " 'And in my arms embrac'd my lass: Warm amidst eternal frost, Too soon the half year's night would pass'. Come here, girl, and hang up some of your things."

"In a moment." She looked up to see the Inspector in the doorway. "We've got a visitor," she called. "Hullo, do come in. I'm Antonia Murray. Sit down, please. Basil won't be long." She passed a hand over her cropped hair. "Sorry to be in such a mess. I was going to change as soon as Basil had finished with the bathroom. What's your dog's name? Shadow." She bent to fondle Shadow's ears.

The Inspector sat down. He had been mistaken in assuming from his earlier brief glimpse that her figure was boylike. In shorts and a bikini top her contours were feminine and delightful. He was apologizing for his intrusion when Basil arrived, buttoning up his shorts.

"My guess was right," he said. "I told Antonia that I thought you might be a policeman—and Carmen confirmed it when we saw her just now."

"Perhaps you were expecting one," the Inspector suggested smilingly. "You may have wondered whether the recent deaths were accidental."

"I'd heard the local gossip but, frankly, didn't pay much attention to it."

"Perhaps you were right not to, Mr Seaton. But we can

return to that point later. What I would be grateful for now is your advice, perhaps I should say your opinion, as an English lawyer." Taking Eldred's will from his pocket, he handed it over. "Can you tell me if this is valid?"

"Yes, it appears to be completely in order," Basil said a minute later. "All former wills revoked, bank appointed as executors, signed, dated and witnessed." He glanced again at the beginning of the document. "Made the day before he died," he commented.

"The day before," the Inspector repeated. "My question is this—If his wife died at the same time as he did, would she inherit?"

"I'm no expert on this subject—my work is mostly in Court—but the rule is that when a husband and wife die simultaneously the elder is deemed to have died first. English law will apply, since both were domiciled in England." Basil folded the will carefully and returned it. "I believe that Eldred was a few years older than Clarice. I'd guess he was in his middle fifties. And I remember her saying here last year that she had no intention of celebrating her fiftieth birthday, since people then immediately began to think of one as old."

"According to his passport he was born in May, 1920. Her passport has not yet turned up, but Colin is looking for it."

"He'd better look among her underclothes. That's where Antonia keeps hers for safety." Basil grinned. "But, to return to what you said earlier, is there a possibility that they may not have died simultaneously?"

"A possibility, yes." The Inspector gave the faintest of hand movements. "No one can say with any certainty at what actual moment either of them died; but the post-mortem findings and other evidence put it beyond reasonable doubt that they died at approximately the same time."

"I see. Well, assuming that is so, Eldred as the elder is deemed to have died first, and Clarice inherited his estate. You should know shortly who her heirs are. I sent a wire on Colin's behalf to her bank, and no doubt they or her solicitors will be writing to him."

"According to Carmen and Miss Clegg she made a similar will on Sunday night leaving everything to her husband. They witnessed both wills." The Inspector repeated what they had told him and the conversation overheard by Thersie. "But until her will is found we shan't know whether she added the codicil."

"Unless it was witnessed and you find the witnesses." Basil paused and, when the Inspector remained silent, went on, "In any case, apart from such a codicil, the position as regards her will is that, although it remains valid, it cannot take effect since Eldred, as the elder, is deemed to have predeceased her. Her property will then pass on as an intestacy."

"You'll have to put that in simpler words for me," the Inspector smiled.

"Sorry. It means that her property passes as if she had died without making a will, and that her estate will be distributed among her next-of-kin in accordance with the relevant Acts."

"So far as Colin is aware, he is the sole next-of-kin."

"Then he's going to be a very well-to-do young man," said Basil, adding dryly, "In the circumstances, if there is suspicion about the manner of their deaths, it's just as well he wasn't here when they occurred."

The Inspector agreed. Then, almost as if he were thinking aloud, he said quietly, "James Rowley died at the same time."

"Yes, he did." Basil picked up a glass of the wine which Antonia had poured out for all of them, then nearly dropped it. For a few seconds he sat completely still, clutching it. "My god!" he exclaimed. "Is that what's in your mind? A murder to cover up two other murders, to close for ever the mouth of the man who saw what happened?"

The Inspector remained silent but attentive, as if he were waiting for the other man to travel the same train of thought.

"Well, well," Basil said at last. "So that's why you wanted to know about the wills. Colin was found on the scene, and no one but he can say how long he'd been there. He seems likely to inherit the estates of both his uncle and aunt. Whether or not the codicil of which you spoke was added would seem irrelevant."

"Have you any reason to think that Colin has not told you the truth?" Antonia demanded abruptly.

"None. He was extremely frank and factual." The Inspector turned to Basil. "Mr Seaton, as a lawyer you will not misunderstand me if I ask where you were between one and three o'clock on Monday."

"Give me a few moments to collect my thoughts." Basil concentrated, then nodded. "I must have been in Gerona, sitting under the trees in what I think is called the Paseo Central, reading the *Vanguardia* and eating some bread and cheese I'd taken with me. I left here fairly early in the morning, about nine, to have another look at the Cathedral and wander round the town. I was, I'd thought, meeting Antonia at Flassá off the train that leaves Port-Bou shortly before half past one; but somehow I'd made a stupid mistake, and she was actually catching the train which reaches Flassá about that time. The result was that she waited an hour and a half for me and was on the point of taking a taxi when I arrived. We stopped at La Bisbal to do some shopping and got here about a quarter to four. The Civil Guard turned up shortly, and Antonia and I went to help in the search for the bodies. As I expect you know, I found James, poor chap, at the same time as Escipión found Eldred."

It was surely unlike Basil, the Inspector reflected as he listened, to have made a mistake about the time of Antonia's train. This was a solicitor trained to note and to remember details. His mind went back to the first time he had seen Basil. "And what have you done since then?" he asked.

"Very little except laze here with Antonia. I sent some telegrams off from Palafrugell on Tuesday. Today I went in again to the chemist's and saw you at the petrol station on the way back. Then, of course, Antonia and I went to the funeral at Palamós. Apart from that, I don't think we've left the place." There was mild amusement in his voice, but a

84

sharpness in his glance, as he added, "I'm sure you don't ask questions without purpose, but I'm darned if I can see what bearing my holiday occupations can have on your inquiries."

"Perhaps none," the Inspector agreed. "But you will have found in your own profession that what may seem irrelevant information can subsequently prove to be of interest." He did not miss the infinitesimal contraction of Basil's left hand from which the mercurochrome had now nearly faded, leaving no trace of the scratch that had been mentioned. What the lips had been prevented from uttering was so often divulged by an involuntary movement of the muscles. The hand, he reflected, held an alphabet, though at times what was spelled could too easily be misinterpreted. But this time the message was plain.

He bade them a courteous adieu. Silence followed his departure and, though he did not look round, he knew that they were staring at each other in question. Why, he wondered, had Basil told him less than the truth? He, like anyone else, might forget to mention an action to which habit had conditioned him, but not something which had so recently occupied some hours of his time.

7

Thursday morning, 14ᵗʰ September

Since breakfast the Inspector had been sitting on the hotel terrace, cogitating and making an occasional entry in a note-book. In the shade of his chair Shadow slept. From time to time a sudden jerk, a ripple of the muscles and a muted whimper indicated that her dreams were not without moments of excitement.

A few yards away the Smurthwaites and the Arkells lay in deck chairs, the aluminium frames of which gave the impression of curving under an unaccustomed weight. He had said "Good morning" when they arrived and received nods of acknowledgement. For a moment he had considered questioning them, but decided that they could have nothing of interest to tell. They were entirely self-absorbed and consequently unobservant: a quartet of dinosaurs who appeared to spend a large part of their time chewing some unimaginative and unimaginable cud. But, come to think of it, hadn't dinosaurs been entirely herbivorous? These four were certainly not. Meat disappeared into their maws like fluff into a vacuum cleaner. At mealtimes their voices were seldom heard except when they were demanding that Bill Eddow, on their behalf, requested 'second helps'. At other times the women discussed with relish the peculiar ailments to which all their friends, without exception, seemed to be subject, and the two men debated the merits of the office machinery from which they made their living.

"I told him he could have thirty per cent off one of them new electrics," Mr Arkell was saying in the high-pitched voice that came so oddly from a man of his bulk. "He said thanks, but he was happy enough with that old Corona he's bashing away on now. Said he'd never used an electric, and at his age didn't see himself learning to."

"Well, maybe he's right there," Mr Smurthwaite observed tolerantly. "Got to catch 'em young to teach 'em anything— like I caught the missus."

The shorter of the two ladies snorted. "If you ever tried to teach me anything, it'd have been something you learned from me." She turned to her companion. "Couldn't even do a Windsor knot on his tie till I showed him."

"Men," said her friend succinctly and, having made her contribution to the conversation, slumped further into her chair.

"Women," grunted her husband. "As I was saying earlier on, Ollie, about those Koppiduplo machines, it's the maintenance and the running costs you've got to look into. Fred and I worked them out close, and I'll tell you we got a surprise. Fred nearly did his nut. I said to him, 'Fred,' I said, 'it's no good going off the deep end. You keep those figures under your hat till I get back.'" His voice droned on.

Putting away his note-book, the Inspector left the terrace. He had reached the Strongitharms' bungalow and noted the closed door and windows when Carmen trotted up, sparkling with health and vitality, a yellow duster in her hand. "It's all right for me to give James's place a bit of a clean-up?" she enquired. "There's bound to be some washing-up and things to be put away."

"I expect so," he agreed. "I'll come with you if I may."

"Thought you might." She looked at him with guileless eyes. "I've got the key in my pocket." She tripped along beside him. "The kids are off my hands for a bit. They're with Miss Clegg; seem to have taken to her. She's good with them too. Pity she didn't marry and have some of her own. Perhaps that's why she took to teaching." She chattered away until they were inside the bungalow. "Stuffy in here, isn't it?" she commented, opening the sitting-room windows and pushing back the shutters.

Together they went round, Shadow padding behind, stopping at intervals to sniff and once, in a dusty corner, to sneeze. In the kitchen a used cup and saucer stood on the marble draining-board; on the stove a small aluminium pan with a scorched plastic handle contained a tablespoonful or two of curdled milk topped by wrinkled skin. One bedroom had not recently been used. In the other and larger bedroom clothes hung on the two chairs and a pair of pyjamas had been flung on the unmade bed. The bathroom shelves bore an assortment of medicine bottles at which the Inspector glanced with casual interest.

Leaving Carmen, the Inspector returned to the sitting-room. It was furnished comfortably but unremarkably except for two antique carved and gilded brackets that flanked a crossed pair of Toledo swords on the wall. The floor of russet-red tiles had recently been waxed and polished. On a large two-pedestal desk, placed so that the light from the window fell over the user's left shoulder, a portable Remington stood uncovered; already a film of dust had dulled keys and metal. Beside it were two orange folio-size folders, each containing some hundred sheets of paper; on the covers had been scribbled in pencil 'Final Revision'. On the wall above the desk two metre-long bookshelves were filled to capacity. A number of works of reference on the lower shelf were within easy reach of anyone sitting at the desk. Glancing along the books, his eye was caught by a title, Clare's *Anatomy of Prison,* a standard work which he hoped, when work allowed, to read. He was opening it, noting Basil Seaton's name on the flyleaf, when a voice he recognized spoke from the doorway. "Hullo. May I come in?"

"Certainly, Mr Warrack." The Inspector returned the book to the shelf. "You wish to speak to me?"

"Well, yes and no." Gregory came smilingly to the desk. "I saw the door open and thought I might seize the chance of looking up something while the maids did my room. I felt pretty sure that James would have a dictionary of quotations

—yes, there it is. Who was it who wrote, 'The truffle is not a positive aphrodisiac—'?"

" 'But on occasion it can make a woman more loving and a man more lovable,' " the Inspector completed the sentence. "I can save you the trouble of looking it up. It was Alexandre Dumas."

"Well, well," Gregory commented admiringly. " 'Ask and it shall be given you.' " He paused. " 'Seek, and ye shall find.' Is it inquisitive to ask whether you are making progress with your inquiries?"

"It's a natural curiosity." The Inspector picked up one of the orange folders and opened it. "You mentioned that Mr Rowley had nearly completed some work. This seems to be it. We must ensure that something is done about it when his affairs are being settled."

"I think I could help you there," Gregory offered. "His agents are also mine. If you wish, I could post the manuscript to them with a covering note. I was going to write to them in any case, so it wouldn't be any trouble to wrap up the MS and send it along."

The Inspector considered before replacing the folder. "I think we should consult the executors first. I'm sure they will wish to do as you suggest, but we mustn't anticipate their decision."

"You're perfectly right; but it can't do any harm to mention the MS to the agents when I write." Gregory looked round the room. "Pleasant little bungalows, these. I'd like to have a place of this sort if the price isn't too high. Poor old James. I think you and he would have got along well together." He frowned slightly. "You know, I've been thinking it was odd that I didn't hear any sound that day. Surely someone must have shouted for help?"

"You were in your room at the hotel at the time, weren't you?"

"I was there all day until Escipión came along with a Civil Guard and asked if I'd help with the search. But I was working—and one tends to be deaf to outside noises if one's engrossed."

"But you broke off for lunch?"

"Not that day. Usually I knock off about two o'clock, get any post there may be and read the paper while I eat an apple or something on the balcony. But last Monday the untying of some knots in the story was going too well for me to stop working, so I skipped lunch and went on without a break until about four."

"You spoke of talking to Mr Rowley about the possibility of collaborating with him on a film script. This conversation was on Sunday?"

"Yes, Sunday night. I mentioned it in the bar, and later in the evening he suggested that we take a stroll and discuss it. If you're asking whether I saw him on Monday, I didn't—until his body was found."

"It was a possibility. He must have passed your window on his way to La Caleta."

"Yes, he must—and other people too. But I'd drawn the blind down—I usually do. It keeps the room cool and the sun off the typewriter keys. I'm not a touch typist. Very few writers are." He looked at his watch, then at the Inspector. "Anything more I can tell you? Then back to work. My room should be ready by now."

From the window the Inspector watched him stride away, stop for a short conversation with Millie and move on to the hotel. Soon Gregory came out onto the balcony of his room, hung a towel on the rail and went inside; then the blind was pulled down.

Carmen, coming into the sitting-room, found the Inspector looking out to sea. Quietly she moved around, emptying an ashtray, fluffing up a cushion, straightening a mat, until he turned. "That's a bit better now," she said. "There's this blue folder marked 'Ideas' that was under his pillow. I'll stick it in here." She opened and closed a drawer, flicked at the typewriter with her duster and, picking up the cover from the floor, snapped it onto the machine. "I'll give the place a good going-over when I've got more time. If you want to stay on, you'd better take the key."

When she had gone he remained standing in thought. He

had a feeling that Gregory had not come in solely to look up a quotation. Possibly he wished to see the bungalow before deciding whether to make an offer to the executors. Taking the *Anatomy of Prison* from the shelf, he tucked it under his arm. Basil would probably be glad to have it back. Closing the shutters and windows, he locked the door behind him.

Connie and Roddie were swimming within a few yards of the beach. Juan, who had just come out of the water, stood watching them critically while he dried his hair with a brown and yellow towel. He nodded as the Inspector joined him.

"They swim well," the Inspector commented.

Juan looked at him unsmilingly. "The sea swallows those who can't swim." After a pause he said, "If I hadn't let the Pooles use the boat they would still be alive."

"Unless someone intended that they should die." The deep voice was without expression.

"Why should anyone wish them dead?" It was more a statement of disbelief than a question.

The Inspector shrugged. "Someone who knew them might be able to suggest a reason."

The children came skipping out of the water, glanced at their father and, interpreting his shake of the head as indication that he did not wish to be interrupted, ran along the sand to the rock against which Miss Clegg was leaning. Juan watched them fling themselves down beside her and raise happily expectant faces. He smiled, then turning to the Inspector, said, "You were asking Carmen what I was doing on Monday morning until I came in for lunch. Do you want me to tell you?"

"If you wish."

"You mean you do." Juan had not missed the deliberately casual tone. "Repairing some bits of furniture, stacking it up for the winter, thinking about women—and wondering if Carmen was keeping my meal hot."

"Did you find the bottle of scent?"

Momentarily Juan was taken aback; then he chuckled. "So she told you about that. Yes, I looked round for it, but she'd already picked it up." He folded the towel carefully, then unfolded it and draped it across his arm. "Are you married?" he asked.

"Yes."

"I don't think you'd have liked to see your wife being kissed by Eldred either," he said—and, for the Inspector, that was sufficient.

Escipión was at the desk in his small office when the Inspector paused at the door. He smiled the patient, wary smile of the hotelier. "You wish to see me?" he queried, lifting a pile of files from a chair.

"If you are not too busy."

Escipión smiled again. No one was ever too busy to talk to the police. But this policeman's courtesy was disarming. "How can I help you, Inspector?"

"I'm trying to build up a picture of last Monday morning from the time the 'Phoebus Abroad' party left: where you were yourself, who else was in the hotel, and whom or what you may have seen."

."I was in here or at the reception desk except for half an hour from ten o'clock when I went to the kitchen to discuss stores and menus with the chef. Mr Eddow went out, I recollect, at about eleven. Then, so far as I can say, apart from myself and the staff—all women except the chef—only Mr Warrack and Miss Best were in the hotel. He was working. I heard his typewriter when I returned from the kitchen. I understand that she was unwell and had said she would be staying in her room."

"Then you saw neither of them?"

"Not Mr Warrack. I saw her cross the foyer in the direction of your room a little after midday."

"Did you see her return?"

"No. But I was in here working on the accounts and I would not necessarily have noticed her." He thought for a moment. "I closed the door later as I did not wish to be disturbed—and I wasn't."

"And you were here until when?"

"Until about twenty past two when I went into the dining-room for lunch. Usually I have a tray brought in here; but when there are no guests lunching I have my meal in there." He raised a shoulder a little. "It keeps the staff on their toes. On Monday there were no guests. Mr Warrack is on *demi-pension*—breakfast and dinner—and Miss Best had sent a message that she did not require any lunch."

A few further questions produced no unexpected information, and the Inspector left. There was probably no one, he reflected, who could confirm Escipión's statement that he had stayed in his office until two twenty; but for Escipión to have assumed that, if he left the hotel, his absence would remain unnoticed was a risk beyond common sense. Millie, however— He stood in thought on the hotel steps. If his conjecture as to where she had been going on Monday and why, was correct, could she be induced to confess?

At this moment Millie was in the dumps. Beryl and Cyril had left her and vanished through the cleft to La Caleta. Bill Eddow had waved a casual greeting as he passed by, and was now talking to Juan outside the Bar Felix. Half an hour ago she had seen Gregory leaving one of the bungalows and had gone to meet him.

"Hullo, Greg. Not working today?" she asked hopefully.

"I'm afraid I am," he said kindly. "I had to break off while my room was being done, and I took the opportunity of checking a reference."

"I thought they did your room while you had breakfast." She did her best to keep him talking.

"They usually do, but today they were late. I must get on with my work now, Millie. See you later."

"This afternoon, Greg?" Appeal was in her eyes, and in every movement of her body a reminder and promise of enjoyment. "If I skip the last course at lunch, can I come and see you? There'll be no one about then."

Inwardly he sighed. "Not today. I've got to think—and I can't think if I'm waiting for you. No one could, my dear."

"Tomorrow, then?"

"At the very first opportunity." He smiled reassurance.

"We leave on Sunday," she said miserably.

"Then we'll make Saturday a memorable day, Millie."

"Is that a promise, Greg?"

"It's a promise." He was on his way before she could muster a detaining question.

Millie returned disconsolately to her beach mat. Instinct told her that in some way she had failed to come up to Gregory's expectations. She picked up a paperback romance she had chosen from the seven novels left behind by previous guests, which Escipión kept on a shelf behind the reception desk. After a few pages she put the book down, and, closing her eyes, gave herself up to the heat of the sun. Half asleep, she became conscious of footsteps stopping and opened her eyes to see the Inspector.

"I hoped to find you by yourself," he said as if this was an unexpected pleasure.

She sat up. She had not seen him so closely before. Now she noticed how sympathetic was the look in the violet eyes. Lovely eyes, she said to herself as, unable to think of any adequate reply, she put out a tentative hand to stroke Shadow's back.

"I think you can help me," he said, sitting down beside her.

"Can I?" She continued to stroke Shadow as the dog lay down between them.

"About what happened here last Monday."

"Me help you?" Millie was surprised and disappointed; but it was nice to be no longer alone. "You mean about those people who were drowned? But I don't know anything about them. I never even spoke to any of them."

"That doesn't mean you can't help me, Millie. I'm sure you can. Tell me, have you heard anyone say that it wasn't an accident?"

"They were all talking about it at dinner, but Bill said it was nothing but gossip, and Miss Clegg said gossip like that was dangerous."

"It is—and the best way of stopping it is to find out what

happened. You were in the hotel at the time. You may have heard someone calling out without realizing what they were saying."

"You mean somebody shouting for help?" She shook her head. "No, I didn't hear a thing. I was in bed all day."

"You never left your room?"

"Not until my friend Beryl came back."

"Weren't you in the hall at midday?"

Millie looked down. "I said I stayed in my room."

"But you were seen in the hall."

She kept her eyes averted. "Who says they saw me?"

"It doesn't matter, does it?" he said mildly. "Would you like to tell me where you were going?"

"I didn't go anywhere," she said with unconvincing persistence.

"Millie, you must tell me the truth." He spoke with kindly persuasion. "There were not many people here on Monday, but it is possible that someone joined Mr Rowley for a short time in La Caleta. It may have been a stranger, but it could have been someone he knew. If you can tell me where any particular person was when those three people drowned, then I shall know whether he could or couldn't have been in La Caleta. But when someone tells me he was alone in his room at the hotel at the time, I cannot be sure that he is telling the truth. He becomes a possible suspect—and it is not pleasant to be a suspect when there are rumours of murder."

Her head remained bent so that he could not see her face. "Who do you mean by someone?" she asked at last.

"Gregory Warrack."

"Greg." She looked at him in astonishment—then slowly a smile spread over her face. So Greg had lied for her sake, to protect her from gossip. And he hadn't told her about it because he knew that she would tell the truth to protect him. And that must be why he wouldn't let her come to his room until her last night at Cala Felix when any talk there might be would be after she'd left. "But he wasn't alone. I was with him," she said almost triumphantly. "I went along just after twelve." With engaging candour she told how, over drinks on Sunday night, they had planned her pretended illness so that she could cry off the tour to Ampurias. "The funny thing is that I wouldn't have gone anyway. I did really have a headache and my tummy felt a bit upset. But Beryl gave me some capsule things and the headache had almost gone when I went along to Greg. She'd said to take one every four hours, so Greg made me have one before we went to bed—and they worked a treat." She drew in her breath. "We had a wonderful time," she murmured as if to herself.

The Inspector smiled inwardly. It was impossible not to believe this pretty, unashamed hedonist; it was impossible not to like her for her honesty. It occurred to him that the human race had many problems which did not trouble the rest of the animal kingdom. The female porcupine, he had been told, was on heat on one day only during the year.

"How long did you stay?" he asked.

"Only about four hours. You see, I had to be in my room before Beryl got back. If I wasn't there, she'd know instead of guessing—and she can't keep things to herself, Beryl can't."

"So you had to keep an eye on the time?"

"We both did. I had my watch on, and there was a clock beside me. The first time I looked it wasn't yet half past one, and the next just over half an hour later. Then we both forgot about time, and it was after four when Greg remembered to look. I didn't want to go, but Greg said we had to get up and," recollection illumined her face, "he carried me into the bathroom and turned on the shower—and I was back in my room by half past four." She stopped abruptly, then looked into his eyes, her expression anxious and pleading. "Look, I've been honest with you. You don't have to let it go any further, do you? I mean I don't want everybody to know about Greg and me. It's not that I'm ashamed of it. I mean, that's why we're made as we are, isn't it? But nasty-minded people make it sound dirty."

"People tell me a great many private things, Millie. I never repeat them unless my duty compels me to."

She listened to the deep, warm voice and knew that she

could trust him to keep his word. "Then that's O.K. I can tell Greg I've told you, can't I, so he won't have to go on making up lies for me?"

"Yes, you can tell him." She would do so, he knew, in any case.

"You're a nice chap." Millie eyed him up and down with approval, then put a hand to her mouth. "Ooh, I shouldn't say that to a policeman."

He smiled. "I'm not only a policeman."

"No, I guess you're not." She was trying to think of some way of prolonging the conversation when Beryl came running towards them followed by a clearly embarrassed Cyril.

"Have you any of those capsules left that you took Monday?" Beryl called from some yards away. "Cyril's got the runs—and they seemed to cure you quick enough."

"I took them back but forgot to leave them," said Millie, who on her last visit to Gregory had purposely retained the bottle. "They're in my dressing-table drawer. There's four or five left. But ought you to take them without asking?"

"Cyril'll ask Greg if he sees him. But he's got another bottle—he said so." She turned to her swain who was shifting from foot to foot behind her. "You pop along, me lad, and get 'em. It's the right-hand drawer, if Millie doesn't mind you seeing what else's in it."

"Why should I?" Millie said shortly. Now she was going to lose her excuse to visit Gregory uninvited. She should have said that she'd returned the bottle. "It's a small bottle, and they're called Bena-something. You shouldn't need to take more than three of them," she added hopefully as Cyril departed at a pace that connoted urgency.

Beryl plumped herself down on one end of Millie's mat. "You having a private chat, or can I join in?" Without waiting for an answer, she turned to the Inspector. "Wish I had a job like yours where I could sit in the sun like you're doing."

"It has its pleasant moments," he acknowledged.

"Want to ask me anything?" Beryl's eyes were bright with curiosity. "Expect I could tell you a thing or two."

"I'm grateful for what you've already told me." He rose. "And now I must leave you."

Beryl gazed after his departing figure. "Now what the hell did he mean by that?"

But Millie wasn't listening. Silently she cursed her friend for the interruption. She felt that the Inspector understood her. It had not been difficult to tell him the truth.

8

Thursday morning and afternoon, 14ᵗʰ September

MILLIE WAS perfectly right. The Inspector had understood her, perhaps better than she realized, and was grateful for her candour. Gregory's presence at Cala Felix at the time of the drownings inevitably made him a possible suspect; but the alibi which Millie provided covered not only the probable time of death but an hour or more on either side of it. He had not found Gregory a sympathetic character, but even positive dislike of a man was no reason to consider him a likely killer.

"Good morning." Miss Clegg's voice, pleasantly tart and crisp like a Ribston Pippin, roused him from contemplation. She was sitting against her private rock, pencil and notebook in hand; her face wore a somewhat mischievous expression. "You really mustn't miss one of the sights of Cala Felix. I'm not going to point, but please look at the hotel terrace."

Obediently he turned. Amazement and amusement conquered his normal self-control. Mrs Smurthwaite and Mrs Arkell had today donned trousers of identical brightly flowered and shiny synthetic material. It was to be assumed that one of them had dropped something, for they were bent double, or as double as their figures permitted, and waddling round peering intently under chairs and tables. No one could deny that the design of the material fully met a demand for psychedelic patterns. Each elephantine blancmange of a behind displayed a matching pair of Greek swastikas within rainbow halos.

"I know one shouldn't laugh," Miss Clegg allowed with unconvincing penitence. "I like wearing trousers myself—I always do when I'm on holiday; but when one is that size one should really avoid them. I don't really know you well enough to ask this, although you did me a favour I shall never forget, but the sight of those incredible rumps so exhilarated my muse that I scribbled down a verse—and it'll be completely wasted unless I can show it to someone else now." With becoming hesitation she proffered her notebook.

In a neat and magnificently legible handwriting he read:

> Ladies, bear this fact in mind:
> Men are foolish but not blind.
> Trousers weren't (and aren't) designed
> For the bulk of womankind.

He chuckled. "Them's my sentiments too," he said.

"As Thackeray wrote," she exclaimed in delight. "You're a man after my own heart, Inspector. You speak admirable English, you're widely read, and your grammar is exemplary."

"My grammar is not my own. I like to think it is that of your classic writers. I am merely a parrot."

"To me a nightingale. When I hear those two women and their husbands talk—which isn't often—it's all I can do to stop myself from correcting them. I'm a born pedagogue."

"And when you hear the Strongitharm brothers talking?"

"I adore them. They contrive to make grammar seem obsolete. When Perce or Jack says 'We was going to do' this or that, I realize that basically it doesn't matter how a man speaks. What matters is the man himself."

"Which means that you would trust them?"

"Unreservedly."

"Even if you found them doing something unethical?"

"You ask difficult questions." She hesitated. "They are pragmatists, but I feel sure they wouldn't do anything unnatural or harmful. Yes, I would trust them with my life."

"Would you trust Basil Seaton similarly?"

"You're quizzing me." She looked away. "I don't think I should offer an opinion about anyone of whom I know so little."

"But you will have formed your own estimate, just as I have formed mine. Let me say this, Miss Clegg. Instinct and experience lead me to think that various people here have not told me the truth, or have told only part of it. I am looking for a possible murderer. I have seen only the faces that have been shown to me. The faces you have seen will not be the same. You will have been able to look at them with complete objectivity because you have not been concerned with the question whether they have lied or whether they have withheld what they do not wish to be known. Have you noticed anything which appears to you to be altogether outside someone's character as you see it?"

"You're asking me to be a village gossip." She chuckled. "Well, here goes. I was frankly surprised to find Basil Seaton staying with, one could say living with, a young woman, a most intelligent and delightful one by the way, whose surname and wedding ring suggest that she could be another man's wife. Yes, I know she may be a widow or a divorcee, but the situation seems uncharacteristic of the man. Although I scarcely know Basil I have often heard a friend of mine who works for the Prisoners' Aid Society speak of him. He does a very great deal for those who have got into trouble with the law, represents them in court and befriends what he calls his 'untouchables' when they come out of gaol. My friend regards him as a man with a mission and of the greatest integrity. I gather that he had a notable war record as an agent in Belgium and Holland. He speaks half a dozen languages fluently. I'd have said he was a Man with a capital M—certainly not a man who would dream of putting a girl's good name in jeopardy. So I'm passing no judgment until I know the facts. But you want to know whether I'd trust him—and the answer is I would. But why should you trust my judgment? In fact, why should you trust me? Am I not, too, a possible suspect?"

"I trust my own opinion of you," he said. "As for the other point, you were at Ampurias with others when the deaths occurred. You were also a stranger to everyone here, to both the living and the dead."

"I was . . ." She looked out to sea and was silent for a while. "I was alone among the ruins at Ampurias from noon, when the others went to the beach. I did not see any of them, or they me so far as I know, until we met again at the bus at about half past four." Abruptly she changed the subject. "You were talking to Millie just now. Am I right in thinking that she made a confession?"

"She did."

"I've got eyes in my head and I don't need a crystal ball to know what she told you. Poor Millie. You know, Inspector, a bird doesn't fly because it has wings, it has wings because it flies. A woman doesn't indulge in sex because Nature has endowed her with the necessary parts; she has them because she's a woman. There is no such thing as an amphigam among human beings, though no doubt," Miss Clegg observed dryly, "science, in its eagerness to improve on Nature, will soon produce one. As it is, some people are born with an organic flaw—one might call them sexual alcoholics, and Millie is one of those. She may not be a good girl in the Puritanical sense, but she's good-hearted and honest. I'm sure what she told you was the unvarnished truth."

"So am I."

"Good. If you had spoken to me before you talked to her I was going to ask you to be gentle with her; but now that I know you a little better I realize that it would have been unnecessary. I suppose that in the absence of an unattached boy of her own age it was inevitable that she should fall into the arms of Gregory Warrack. A kinder man might not have taken advantage of her accessibility, but," she went on dryly, "few men are as kind as that, and Gregory is the complete egoist, unimaginative and without compassion—though he can be very good company." With a return to brusqueness, she continued, "Now I've gossiped enough—too much. I'm a meddler by nature. If I had half a dozen grandmothers I'd be teaching the lot how to suck eggs. I'm going for a walk. No, don't offer to come with me. You can occupy your time more profitably." Before the Inspector could utter she was ten yards away, striding out as if she were in training for a marathon walk. Watching her go, he was conscious that a minute earlier she had been about to take him into her confidence, but that for some reason, perhaps an inability to discuss personal matters, she had changed her mind.

Carmen was rubbing a duster over the counter when the Inspector went into the Bar Felix. "Going to be here much longer?" she asked as she poured out the lemonade he requested.

He gave a shrug. "Why do you ask?"

"Curiosity, I s'pose." She leaned her elbows on the counter. "Of course I don't know a thing, but, honest, I can't see anyone here doing those people in. I mean they're all decent folk. Yes, what is it, Juan?" she asked as her husband came in and muttered to her.

"I'm going into town to pick up the grill from the blacksmith. He said I could have it on Thursday. Anything you want?"

"Not for myself, but I told you last night to ring Ernesto about the money. You and your ruddy cadging friends," she said irately. "He's owed us for six months, and the note Bill brought back said he'd be along with it the next day which was Tuesday. So see you ring him and say if he doesn't pay up this week I'll come along myself and sort him out."

"What's his number?"

"Oh, look it up in the book," she told him impatiently. "It's 314 something—wait a mo., it's on his letter." She took a folded paper from the shelf behind her. "314989. Here, stick it in your pocket, then you won't forget. Off you go now, and don't be back late or your dinner'll be cold." She gave him a wifely push before turning to the Inspector. "Perce said to remind you that whenever they went diving you were welcome to come along. They're out in the launch now with Bill, after some more pictures. You wouldn't have thought, would you, that they were the kind to go in for that sort of thing, photos of fish and bits of seaweed and the like. Just shows you can never tell about people." She chatted away until the Inspector finished his drink.

Going to the hotel, he heard the rat-tat of Gregory's typewriter as he went down the passage to his room. From the half-open door of the linen cupboard came a voice redolent of gossip. "There was lipstick on the pillow by the window when I turned down the bed last night," Montserrat was saying. "I expect she'll be along today."

Poor little Millie, the Inspector said to himself. Her *affaire* is public property.

"There's one I'd fancy more myself," Teresa said, "and that's this pol—" She stopped abruptly and jammed a hand against her lips as the Inspector pushed the door open. His expression reassured her that he had heard nothing. Leaning against the door post, he apologized for interrupting their work. "I wanted to ask whether either of you saw anyone coming into or leaving the hotel on Monday while the tour party was at Ampurias."

"*Señor* Eddow went out about eleven," Teresa volunteered.

"Did you see *Señor* Rowley as he went to La Caleta?"

Montserrat shook her head. "We were all of us talking about him in the kitchen that night. We hadn't seen him or anyone else. The bedrooms were all done early, and you don't see the beach from anywhere else but the hall."

Hopefully the Inspector questioned them further. For, with suspicion of murder, the vampire bat of gossip spreads its wings—and gossip is a sharp spur to recollection as well as to invention. But, when he left them, he had learned nothing that he did not already know except that Montserrat's *novio* was doing his military service and that Mr Arkell—surprisingly—slept in a nightshirt.

Before, during and after lunch he sat in thought, running through the entries in his note-book and marshalling his ideas. Statements had been made that could and must be checked.

When the Post Office in Palafrugell opened in the afternoon he was there. Twenty minutes later he copied two telegrams into the note-book and, borrowing the local telephone directory, ran his eye down the listed numbers until he found what he was looking for. Then, after using the telephone, he took the road to Palamós, Shadow erect, nose at window, by his side.

Thersie and Colin had searched the bungalow thoroughly during the morning and found nothing of interest except a partly burned scrap of paper lodged in a crevice between two bricks in the hearth; it was a heavy ledger paper that looked to them very like that of Eldred's will which the Inspector had taken with him. Then they went to swim, to lie on the beach and to talk. On their return it occurred to Thersie to look in the Pooles' car, and there in the glove pocket she found Clarice's passport.

Now, having lunched on the terrace, they were washing up.

"You know, I can't think that your aunt would have burned the will unless she had made a new one," remarked Thersie.

"You didn't know her." Colin smiled. "She was a spur-of-the-moment person."

"Well, I think we might have another look. I've often found things where I'd already searched—and it's usually in the most likely place. You're sure it couldn't be in the desk?"

"Not in the drawers I went through. I turned everything out. The Inspector searched the other drawers, and I can't see him overlooking anything. But you're right, it's the obvious place. Shall we go through the lot together?" He hung up the tea towel and followed her into the sitting-room. "Be careful when you pull out that top drawer. It's full to bursting."

The drawer came out smoothly three-quarters of the way; then there was resistance. As Thersie slid in a hand to press down the contents they heard a rustle of paper and the sound of something slipping to the bottom of the tier.

"Wait a moment." Colin knelt and, pulling out the bottom drawer, stretched his arm to reach the back panel and brought out an envelope and some crumpled sheets of paper. Smoothing a sheet, he exclaimed, "You were right, Thersie. It's a will."

She knelt beside him to read.

It was immediately plain that Clarice had copied the wording of the stationer's standard form. In her backward sloping hand she had written:

This is the Last Will and Testament of me Clarice Huntingdon Poole of the Old Grange Cogleigh in the County of Sussex made this [a space had been left for the date] day of September one thousand nine hundred and seventy-two and I hereby revoke all former Wills and Testamentary Dispositions of any kind at any time heretofore made by me and I appoint the Capital and Counties Bank (Hereinafter called my Trustees) to be the Executors and Trustees of this my Will. I bequeath the sum of Ten

That she had been interrupted in the course of writing and had hastily pushed the paper into the drawer seemed evident.

Thersie sat back on her haunches. "I suppose that was the ten thousand she wanted you to have. It doesn't look as if you'll get it now."

"I don't mind whether I do or not." Colin got up and pulled Thersie to her feet. "No, that's not quite true. No one would refuse a sum like that, but I shan't worry if I never receive it. I'm doing work I enjoy and I can live happily on my salary. I don't need anything more."

The words "Don't you?" were in her mind, but what she said was, "I'm glad," and to Colin her smile was nothing but a smile.

"Thank heavens we don't have to do any more searching," he said. "I'll put everything into an envelope and we can take it along to the Inspector—and then we're free. What shall we do?"

"Swim, and then drive somewhere for dinner. Dutch

106

treat."

"Dutch be damned. If I don't pay we don't go."

"All right," said Thersie meekly. I'll ask him to drive to-night, she told herself. I hope he drives well.

The Inspector, Escipión said when they reached the hotel, had gone out in his car. The envelope could be kept in the safe until his return. Scribbling a note about the part-burnt scrap of paper, Colin handed it over.

"But it's not a police matter that I owe Juan a little money." Ernesto had been surprised and shocked when the Inspector introduced himself and mentioned the debt. "He rang me this morning, and I told him I would bring it to-morrow."

"It's not the money that interests me," the Inspector said, "but the reason why you put your letter to Juan in the launch last Monday instead of handing it to whoever was in charge of the boat."

"I saw *Señor* Eddow tie up and go to a café, and I wrote a note for him to give to Juan. But when I reached the café he was sitting with a man to whom I do not speak, a bad man, a *Señor* Rojais."

"You mean this man had done you some injury?"

"Injury." Ernesto spat the word. "He turned my daughter into a prostitute. He has done many other evil things." Anger and a wish for revenge loosened Ernesto's tongue. The Inspector listened in silence. Ernesto needed no prompting. If Rojais were guilty of a tenth of the crimes of which he was now being accused, then his after-life would indeed be spent among fire and brimstone.

When the Inspector left Ernesto, he paid a visit to the headquarters of the Civil Guard; then, going towards the quay, he came to a bench on which three aged men, each grasping a stick with gnarled hands, sat in desultory conversation. Here he might find what he sought—here on *El Banco de Si-No-Fuera,* where those whose working lives are over reminisce about the 'might-have-been'— "If it had not been for the great flood . . . for the lack of rain . . . for my daughter's marriage to that good-for-nothing . . . if . . . if . . . if . . ." He said "Good afternoon" with such friendliness and diffidence at disturbing them that they shuffled along to let him sit. A few words about the weather and the fishing prospects, and he came to his question.

"No, *señor,* I regret that we cannot help you." The least bowed of the three shook his head, adding with a smile devoid of amusement, "We were all in other parts of Spain during the revolution—" he corrected himself dryly "—during the Crusade of Liberation. But there are several men who were here until the end and who survived what followed. One of them is a cousin of mine. He is crippled with rheumatism and unable to leave the house. He would be very happy to have a visitor and to talk about the past."

Talking was the old man's solace, as the Inspector found when he reached the given address. The effort to rise from the cane chair proved too great; the extended hand was shaky and knobbed by arthritis, but the eyes gleamed when he spoke of the days when he was young and active.

He well remembered the launch that had gone down near Cap Tabal in 1937 and the Englishman who captained it. "He was a friend of mine and of many others here, a good man and a brave one. After he lost his boat he came here and stayed with me—I had my own fine house then—until he went back to England. He wrote to me on his return. I have kept his letter all these years." With fumbling fingers he took an ancient wallet from his pocket and extracted a frayed envelope. "Please read it, *señor.* I cannot read myself, but I know what it says by heart."

Carefully the Inspector withdrew the letter. Where the paper was folded it was beginning to part, and the ink had faded to a dull brown; but the writing, large and bold, remained legible. It was a letter of thanks and heart-felt gratitude, offering generosity for generosity. "An unusual surname," he observed when he finished reading and had made the expected appreciative comments.

"It was a barbaric name which none of us could pronounce. We called him Estrón." The old man's head nodded.

"He was a man you could love and trust," he muttered, and the next moment was asleep and gently snoring. To his daughter, who came as if she had been awaiting this signal, the Inspector made his adieux, promising a further visit if he were in the neighbourhood.

Forty minutes later he drove into the dusty approach to Flassá station. There, talking in the shade of the pollarded limes on the platform, he was able to establish that a young lady who answered to his description of Antonia had arrived on Monday by the omnibus train from Port-Bou and had waited for perhaps an hour and a half before a tall man with a scar on his bald head arrived in an English car to collect her. After taking a cup of coffee in the station *cantina* under the cold eyes of the stuffed fox behind the counter, the Inspector returned to Cala Felix, stopping at Luis' shop to buy matches. There he found Beryl paying for a dress which she had had cleaned and pressed. She was complaining loudly and, so far as Luis was concerned, unintelligibly, about the amount she was being charged.

"They don't half stick it on the prices here," she said when he had translated her complaint without result. "Thanks for your help all the same." She winked broadly at him as she went off. "Millie's taken a fancy to you," she called.

Pocketing the matches, the Inspector looked round the shop while he waited for his change. Shelves and wire racks held the remains of the season's stocks of wines, spirits, tinned foods, packeted biscuits and odds and ends. Bread, rolls, fruit and vegetables were brought in daily, Mondays excepted, when Juan or sometimes Carmen drove to market. A film of dust on the non-perishable articles bespoke Luis' innate laziness which was confirmed by the heavy stubble on the discontented face and lack of lustre in the brown eyes over which epicanthic folds of the lids hinted at dilution of the vigorous blood of Cataluña.

Through an open door at the back of the shop could be glimpsed the two gleaming machines in which Pura dealt with the laundry and clothes-cleaning required by visitors.

The loaded lines of washing which were daily to be seen at the back of the building showed that, whatever her state of health, she did not neglect her work.

A few questions were sufficient to establish that neither Luis nor his wife, who came in response to her husband's shout, could give him any information about last Monday. One negative fact, however, emerged: that Luis, alone among the men whom he had interviewed, neither bathed nor swam.

Returning to the hotel, he read the note from Colin which Escipión gave him and, going to his room, opened the accompanying envelope. A comparison of the scorched scrap of paper with Eldred's will left little doubt that the former had been part of Clarice's witnessed will—or, at any rate, part of a similar will-form. Her passport had been issued the previous year. It was with surprise and interest that he noted the date of her birth, the 12th January, 1920.

9

Late afternoon, Thursday, 14ᵗʰ September

Oɴ ᴛʜᴇ ᴛᴇʀʀᴀᴄᴇ of his bun-
galow Basil sat reading. Beside his deck chair lay a scatter of
folded maps and a pile of guide books. He welcomed the
Inspector and Shadow warmly. "Antonia's washing her
hair," he said. "And I'm considering writing a new kind of
guide, drawing on the experiences of my friends and myself.
It will be called *Where not to Stay or Eat in Europe.* When
it's completed I propose to take a year off and visit all the
places I'm naming. I think I should get free accommodation
and all the very best food that the chefs reserve for their
families in exchange for an undertaking to remove the relevant entry from my book. Of course I should put on a good
deal of weight during the tour, but a spell in prison for at-
tempted extortion should deal adequately with that problem." He chuckled. "Now, what can I do for you? For I'm
sure that it's not the charm of my company alone that brings
you here."

"Give me some further advice before you go to gaol." The
Inspector sat down. "You told me yesterday that when a
husband and wife die, so far as is known simultaneously, the
elder will be presumed to have died first. We were then
under the impression that Clarice was some years younger
than her husband, and it seemed likely that Colin would
benefit very considerably by their deaths. But Clarice's passport has now been found, and she proves to have been a few

months older than Eldred."

"You surprise me—you do indeed." Basil reflected. "Well, in that case, she will be presumed to have died first, and her will takes effect. If I remember aright you said that it was in identical terms to Eldred's will, which means that, subject to any codicil, her entire property passes to him. But *his* will leaving his estate to *her* cannot take effect because she is deemed to have predeceased him. His property, therefore, which now includes hers, again subject to any codicil, passes as on an intestacy."

"Which means that *his* next-of-kin will inherit?"

"Provided they come within certain stated classes of relatives. If there should prove to be none of those, then the Crown snatches the lot. As Shakespeare said, the Crown is 'like a deep well that owes two buckets filling one another; the emptier ever dancing in the air'. Its thirst is unquenchable."

"As is a Republic's." The Inspector smiled before asking, "If there were a relative, the son of a divorced mother by a second husband, would he fall within any of those classes?"

"You do ask the most unusual questions." Basil rubbed his jaw. "My inclination is to say 'yes'; in fact, I'm fairly sure the answer is 'yes'. He'd have to go through certain legal formalities to claim his inheritance, but I don't think there'd be any particular problem involved."

"But there *is* a problem of quite another colour." The Inspector produced the singed piece of paper, Eldred's will and the part-written will of Clarice, and added a succinct explanation.

"Well, well." Basil's eyebrows rose. "If your conjecture that Clarice burned her witnessed will is right and if there is no other will in existence, the situation alters. As I said, this kind of thing is outside my usual run—but I think this is where we come to a joker in the intestacy pack. The rule I told you about was to some extent amended in 1952. Without going into a lot of legal verbiage, it means that Eldred will be deemed *not* to have survived Clarice. And as she will be deemed not to have survived him—" He let the sentence die. "I suppose you want me to tell you what's likely to happen to both estates. I *think* each estate would pass to the respective next-of-kin. In Clarice's case that would seem to mean Colin and anyone else who qualifies; in Eldred's, if there's only one qualifying next-of-kin, the whole lot goes to him. That's what I *think,* but if I were the lawyer concerned —and thank God I'm not—I'd take Counsel's Opinion." He lay back with a sigh of relief as Antonia came out carrying a tray.

"I heard you two talking away and guessed you could do with a drink." She gave them each a glass and sat down, running fingers through her still-damp hair. "Now," she demanded, "what were you talking about?"

"Wills, intestacies and inheritance," said Basil. "Subjects on which I'm prepared to instruct you in due course if we can find nothing else to talk about."

Opening his note-book, the Inspector passed it to Basil. "Does this mean anything to you?" he asked.

" 'BULLSEYE TUESDAY NOON SOLE MEUN-IERE'," Basil read aloud. "What on earth is it? An instruction to a chef?"

"The whole of a telegram bar the signature." The Inspector sipped at his glass. "What does the word 'bull's-eye' mean to you?"

"Is this a Freudian test? No. Well, the first thing that came into my head was the striped peppermint sweet I used to suck as a kid. Gob-stoppers the big ones were called— about this size." He formed a rough circle with finger and thumb. "My father used to give me one to stop me chattering when he was trying to think. To a so-called sporting man, which I'm not, it would mean a shot that hits the centre of the target or the centre itself—what archers like my brother call a 'gold'. It's a kind of lantern, too; something to do with the convexity of the glass, I think. It's also some sort of pulley—and a little round window. I expect there are other meanings. I've an idea it was a slang term for some coin."

The Inspector nodded. "And *sole meunière?"*

"Oh, the best way of cooking my favourite fish. It suggests Dover and lemon—"

"And clarified butter—and a restaurant like Madame Prunier or Wheelers," added Antonia. "And—oh, a bottle of Montrachet. That's what we'll have, Basil, when we go back to London."

The Inspector smiled at her manifest happiness; then, "May I look at your Michelin?" he asked. He took the book from Basil, rapidly turned the pages, paying particular attention to one. Closing it, he said, "I would like to go back, Mr Seaton, to something you told me last night. You said, if I remember correctly, that since Monday morning you had driven to Gerona, to Palamós for the funeral, and twice to Palafrugell."

Basil assented.

"When I saw you at the petrol station I gathered that you had had your tank filled on Monday morning. Do you recall how many litres were put in?"

"Forty."

"And you had the same quantity on Wednesday. It would seem that your car is using a quite astonishing amount of petrol—or, perhaps more likely, that you have omitted to tell me of some other journey, or possibly made a rather longer journey than you mentioned."

Basil was listening politely, almost as if he were waiting for the speaker to reach the point of an anecdote which so far had little intrinsic merit.

"It was a conversation about a tip given by Carmen to a telegraph boy which led me to make inquiries at the Post Office. I won't apologize for overhearing—it was impossible not to do so. It occurred to me that this telegram might possibly account for the journey you failed to recall. I looked through the copies of telegrams received and sent, and found two that interested me. One you have already helped me to interpret. The other was one that you yourself received." He turned the pages of the note-book. " 'VIVALDI DUE MATARO MONDAY ELEVEN HOURS GLAUBER BEARER' ", he read aloud. "I rang Mataró and found that a ship under charter called the *Antonio Vivaldi* called there on Monday, loaded and unloaded some cargo and sailed for Marseilles later in the day. Now, Mr Seaton, did you go to Mataró to meet someone on that ship?"

Basil sat for a while, his gaze turned inwards; then he looked at Antonia. Whatever it was that he saw in her face decided him, and he suddenly grinned. "All right. Wasn't it Mark Twain who said 'When in doubt, tell the truth'? I'll tell you exactly what I did and, if I have to go to prison, I hope Antonia will bring me some decent food. First, I must explain that my work brings me into close contact with a number of people who have fallen foul of the law, petty offenders as well as criminals, and that many of the former and some of the latter have become my very good friends. I therefore have quite a lot of information given to me in confidence.

"Now, however bad law-breakers may be, there are several forms of crime which most of them won't condone; one of them is child-rape, another drug-running. This telegram you have unearthed was sent to me by an old friend and ex-gaol-bird. He had heard through the grapevine that a member of the *Vivaldi*'s crew, a Frenchman called Glauber, was bringing a parcel of heroin from Turkey. He let me know. What action I was to take was up to me, but my duty as a responsible citizen was obvious."

"Even more obvious to a lawyer," the Inspector said with a smile.

"Doubly so," Basil agreed. "But there were other considerations. If I told the local Civil Guards, would they believe me? It would be difficult to explain the situation without naming my informant—who naturally wishes to remain anonymous. If they did believe me, they might decide to search the ship and, if they found the heroin, arrest Glauber. Or they might allow Glauber to proceed to Marseilles, the next and final port of call, and notify the French police. If he were arrested at Mataró, then the opportunity of tracing those for whom he acted as carrier would be lost. If he were to be allowed to go on to Marseilles, the decision would have

115

to be made by your narcotics people, and there might well have been considerable delay while the appropriate officials were consulted. And, if the ship's departure were held up, Glauber would certainly begin to worry and quite possibly get rid of the heroin." Basil paused briefly. "That's what went through my mind. What decided me to do what I did was my doubt that I'd be believed. Just suppose that a Spanish tourist came into a police station in a small English port with such a story; I can imagine that it would take some time to convince the station-sergeant that he wasn't a nut case."

An odd story, the Inspector reflected, perhaps odd enough to be true. "What then did you do?" he inquired.

"I was at Mataró when the *Vivaldi* arrived. I went aboard at once, saw the Captain, told him of my suspicions and allowed it to be assumed that I was connected with our narcotics people. Fortunately I speak Italian fluently, and I succeeded in convincing him of my authority. No search of the ship was to be made, I said; what I had told him was not to be repeated to anyone; if Glauber had any particular friends aboard, their names were to be given to the French police who would come aboard at Marseilles. When I left, I telephoned a friend in Marseilles and asked him to pass the information on to the police. It was waiting for that call to go through which made me so late in meeting Antonia at Flassá." His fingers traced the outline of the scar on his head, and he said with finality, "That's the truth, the whole truth and nothing but the truth, believe me."

"I should be glad to," the Inspector said blandly. "Why did you not tell me the truth yesterday?"

"Because I hoped you'd be satisfied with what I did tell you," Basil answered frankly. "I had acted in breach of the law and could scarcely have expected you to overlook it."

"And what do you expect now?"

"My deserts," Basil said soberly.

"Those may depend on whether you have now told me the truth. If the Marseilles police confirm that they received your message—" he looked directly into the other man's

116

eyes "—that may be sufficient."

"Sufficient for what?" asked Basil.

"To confirm me in my opinion." The Inspector's tone was not unfriendly. He turned to Antonia who had been listening and watching intently. "How much of what Mr Seaton has now told me did you already know?"

"All of it." She appeared surprised at the question.

He nodded and, though the expression on the controlled face did not alter, it seemed to both listeners that he was not entirely displeased. Shortly, with a non-committal "Good night," he left them. As he reached the road he saw Colin leaving the Pooles' bungalow and went to meet him.

"He was as friendly as ever." Colin was telling Thersie about his conversation with the Inspector. "He said that, if I had a few minutes to spare, he would like to refresh his memory. I had to go through the whole of Monday morning again; what time I'd left Torroella; how fast I normally walked; when I had first come in sight of La Caleta—in fact, right up to the time you arrived. Then he asked who had found the burnt scrap of the will form, and I said I had. We went back to the bungalow and I showed him the crevice in the hearth. It was then it occurred to me that he might be wondering whether Aunt Clarice had herself burned it or whether it could have been burned after her death. He asked me if my uncle had ever said anything to suggest that they had some sort of phobia about making their wills, and I said that the subject had never come up. Then quite suddenly he thanked me and went off, leaving me wondering."

"Wondering exactly what?" she asked.

"I don't really know." Colin hesitated. "I expect I'd been reading into his questions something that wasn't really there. He was probably only checking to ensure that I hadn't left anything out of my previous account. I'm sure he can't suspect me of having anything to do with anyone's death. I know I hadn't."

"And I know, too," she said with quiet emphasis.

"You do?" He sounded so delighted, almost surprised, by

117

her declaration of faith that she was deeply touched. "But you've only known me since Monday," he muttered as if to himself.

She nodded as if nothing more needed to be said and lay back in her chair, looking at him through half-closed eyes. "I had a letter from Mummy today. They expect to be here on Saturday afternoon. I'm sure you'll get on well with Daddy." She smiled. "You can always tell with him. If he smokes his pipe and says very little, he's accepted you. If he makes a lot of small talk and lets his pipe go out, he's still making up his mind."

"And if he decides he doesn't like me?"

"He'll remember he has a letter to write, shake your hand warmly and murmur that he hopes to see you again one day."

Colin laughed. "And your mother?"

"Oh, she and I usually like the same people." She opened her eyes, then looked away.

Some time later she reached for her handbag and, taking out a paper tissue, gently rubbed it across his lips.

"'Lo." Jack finished tightening the clamp on a lacquered camera housing and put it down on the table. "Come along in and take the weight off your feet." He waved towards a wicker chair. "We was looking for you earlier on."

"There was something that you wanted to tell me?" The Inspector sat down and looked round the room, noting the sturdy, serviceable furniture and the surprisingly tidy condition in which the present tenants kept the place.

"Nah. Told you the lot yesterday. We'd hoped you might be able to take an hour or two off and come out with us. Took Bill instead. He can manage a boat all right, but he's a bit slow on the uptake. Should have got some goodish pictures, though. Water was clear as what comes out of a tap."

"I imagine you've taken a great many photographs since you've been here," the Inspector observed casually.

Jack agreed. "Gives the kids something to look at in the winter and keeps 'em off the telly. Perce and me puts on a

118

show now and then at some of the schools. He does the projecting, and I'm up on my feet doing the spiel."

"You know something about marine life, then?"

"Something's the word. Just about enough to keep the kids from asking me what I don't know."

"You must miss the friend whose boat you were using before you went south."

"Bob. Yes, he knew his stuff. We wouldn't have had him in the family if he didn't. Thought we'd told you he was our brother-in-law. He's taking the boat back over France, canals and all that. Spends all his spare time on the water, does Bob—though it's donkey's years since he's tasted any." He chuckled as glasses clinked in the kitchen. "That'll be Perce out there."

Heavy footfalls, and Perce came in. "Heard you yacking away," he said jovially, plonking down glasses and a large bottle of beer on the table.

"I was telling him about Bob. Ought to be half way home by now if he hasn't rammed a lock. If our friend here wanted to say anything he ain't hardly had a chance to open his mouth."

The Inspector watched them drain their glasses. "I thought you would be interested in something I came across today," he observed. "I believe your father's name was Samuel."

"Ay, but there was nobody called him anything but Sam."

"I was talking today to an old fisherman in Palamós. He told me about a launch which sank not far from here during what you call our Civil War. It seems that it must have gone down near the spot where you were diving before you left here on Monday. It occurred to me that you might have come across the wreck."

"Not me," said Jack.

"Nor me." Perce shook his head vigorously. "Keep away from wrecks is my motto. You can do yourself a bit of no good on chunks of rusty metal. Best to leave them be. Pal of mine nearly lost his brace and bit mucking around a wreck —and on his honeymoon, too," he added with a chuckle.

"Don't expect there'd be much left of a boat which went down all those years back. You must get some pretty rough seas round these parts winter and spring."

The Inspector agreed. "There were four people on board. Three of them were drowned, but one managed to swim ashore—the captain. He was a friend of the old fisherman, an Englishman and quite a well known character. I gathered that he was engaged in gun-running."

"If he had guns aboard, there won't be much of them left now," observed Perce.

"He wasn't carrying guns on this trip—except possibly for self-protection. He'd been hired by a rich industrialist to take himself and his wife to France. The fourth member of the party was a sailor." The Inspector paused. "The cargo was an unusual one—though perhaps not so unusual in those times."

Jack's "Uh" was on an interrogative note.

"It was the industrialist's fortune, or as much of it as was readily portable."

"Getting out while the going was still good. Well, I can't say as I blames him." Perce gestured. "Maybe I'd have done likewise if I'd been him. Not that it did him much good, with them both goners and the stuff at the bottom of the sea."

"I think it might not be."

"Where else could it be?" asked Jack.

"That's where I hoped you might be able to—advise me." The Inspector's voice was blandly hopeful. "The captain who, as I mentioned, was able to swim to shore, stayed with the old fisherman for a time before returning to England. He wrote later to thank him and to offer help whenever needed. The old man kept the letter. He showed it to me." The violet eyes passed from face to face. "It was signed Sam Strongitharm."

In the ensuing silence it seemed to the Inspector that the brothers resolutely refrained from looking at each other. "Well," exclaimed Jack at last. "That fair beats the band, don't it? It's queer about it being the same name, but it couldn't have been our dad, not by a long chalk. He was never out of England until the war, and he spent most of that on the Atlantic or in it. Got torpedoed three times, he did."

"You're sure he never left England?"

"Sure as eggs is eggs," Perce said positively.

"When were you born?"

"'35—and Jack in '36."

"Then I doubt whether either of you can remember where your father was in 1937."

"Must be that we just remember him telling us—and when Dad told you anything, if you didn't take it as Gospel he marked it up on your backside."

The Inspector smiled despite himself as he opened his note-book. "I believe one of you sent a telegram last Monday to Strongitharm, Bright's Hotel, Folkestone—presumably a relation."

"The missus," Perce acknowledged.

"Perhaps you would tell me what it means." The Inspector passed the note-book across the table.

Perce studied the open page. "Looks a bit of a puzzle, don't it? But wires come expensive, so I cut it short as I could. The missus'd understand it O.K. " 'Bull's-eye' tells her that we'd picked the right place here and was enjoying ourselves. The rest of it says we'd be with her Tuesday—that's Tuesday of next week o' course—and what she's to see that we get for our midday dinner."

"I see." But the tone did not express understanding. "Your wife is on holiday at Folkestone?"

"Her and Jack's missus and the kids. They didn't fancy coming abroad. Minnie, that's my missus, has a notion that the water ain't safe to drink and that the kids won't take to the food. So they pushed us off with their love, and popped off themselves to Folkestone."

"I see," the Inspector said once more. "I should have asked to see your passports," he mentioned apologetically after a short pause. "Perhaps I may see them now."

With a sidelong glance at his brother Jack rose and went out, returning shortly. The Inspector riffled through the passport pages. "It would seem from the visa stamps that

you crossed to England from Calais last Tuesday and returned the same day. I hope you all enjoyed your lunch, at
the *À la Sole Meunière*. The Guide Michelin rates it as a
good restaurant."

Perce eyed him thoughtfully, then gave a chuckle. "He's
got us by the short hairs, eh, Jack?"

"Seems he has," Jack agreed soberly. "Will you tell him
—or me?"

"Might as well be me—but I could do with a wet first. Get
us another bottle, will you, Jack?" He sat in thoughtful silence until his glass had been filled, emptied it and passed
the back of his hand across his mouth. "I've got to hand it to
you," he said to the Inspector, "the way you worked things
out. Fancy you spotting that restaurant name in the wire and
finding out where it was. You got the missus beat—and what
she can't see with her back turned ain't worth knowing.
You're right enough about it being our dad that was out here
in '37." He picked up the glass that Jack had refilled and
drank slowly.

"He was a bloody fine engineer, was our dad," he resumed. "Worked with Thornycrofts—and what he didn't
know about boats and engines you could put on the back of
a Green Stamp. Had a proper bee in his bonnet about poli-
tics, though. Always off to labour meetings and the like.
And when your Civil War started and the Huns and the
Eyties came in, it didn't take Mum long to guess what was
in his mind. 'I'm off,' he said to her one night—and the next
day he was. It was all of fifteen months afore she saw him
again.

"Like you said, he was running guns and other things into
these parts. He stayed until he saw what was happening and
made up his mind he wasn't fighting for what he hisself
believed in. I'm not saying he was right or wrong—but
things looked different then to a lot of folk. He made that
last run in the launch because he was being well paid for it,
and he wanted to bring back enough to make up to Mum for
the slaving she'd had to do to keep us kids fed and decent
while he was away. He came back with nowt but the clothes

on his back—and Mum had to chuck 'em in the ash-can. The launch, the other three folk in it and the cargo, a right lot of gold he said, went down. He talked on about going one day to have a look for it, and he died ten years back still talking."

"So you decided to look for it yourselves." It was not a question.

Perce nodded. "But we had to wait till we had the time and the money and some proper training in diving. Costs a lot, this diving lark, and we needed a biggish car to take all the stuff. Well, we're toolmakers, Jack and I, and we make good money, but we wanted the best diving gear there was— and we got it. Dad had left a map showing where the launch sank—he knew this coast like he knew the moles on Mum's back—and the depth at which it ought to be found if it was still there. And we found it right enough. But someone had been there before us, and there wasn't nothing but bits of rusted metal. So we packed up and sent off the wire to say we was on our way."

"And to ask your families to meet you at Calais?" The Inspector's eyebrows rose fractionally.

"Well, in for a penny if we couldn't have the pound, as you might say." Perce winked. "We hadn't got the gold, but we thought we'd take back something to help pay for the trip. So we got a dozen cases of brandy, wrapped 'em up in sacks and shoved them in the back of the car. Then we loaded the compressor and chucked in some diving kit and a lot of other stuff on top. After that it was like spreading butter. The Customs this end looked at the G.B. plates and waved us through—and at Calais by the time we'd loaded up with the fam'ly and what they'd bought I'll tell you that the car looked a proper Christmas tree. When we got over to the other side of the Channel we set the kids to having a good old row, and Minnie gave the baby a pinch and had it screaming just like one of them pop singers. The Customs bloke took one look at us, said he reckoned the baby could do with a dose of gripe-water and the sooner we got home the better."

The smuggler's 'Open Sesame', the Inspector reflected with amusement: a shrieking baby. It was an old trick; but add a couple of honest-faced men with harassed wives and squabbling children, a car piled with diving-gear, kids' toys and French market produce, and who was going to suspect more than the venial smuggling of a few cigars or a bottle over the odds? But—? "What made you come back here after you'd returned to England?" he asked.

"Wanted some more of what we came here for—photos, I mean." Perce grinned. "Keeps the womenfolk quiet as well as the kids when they've got something to look at. 'Sides, we'd left quite a bit of our clobber here."

"And of course you could repeat your smuggling success?"

"Not us. A bottle each next time—what the Customs allows." Perce assumed an expression of virtue unfairly aspersed, then cocked a shameless wink. "You don't have to let on about what we took back last time, do you?"

The Inspector rose. "Not about the—brandy," he said with the ghost of a smile. At the doorway he turned. "I assume that what you smuggled has been safely disposed of?"

"The whole blooming lot," Jack confirmed. "Perce and me didn't keep nothing. We sticks to things what we're used to—like beer."

10

Thursday evening,
14th September

THOUGHTFULLY THE INSPEC-
TOR walked down to the sea. He did not for a moment
believe the story that Perce and Jack had told. It was, to say
the least, unlikely that they had taken the long return trip to
England merely to smuggle a few cases of brandy. Perce's
explanation of the word 'bull's-eye' bore an unconvincing
stamp of quick-witted thinking. If the wrecked launch had
carried a substantial sum in gold it would probably have
been in the form of bars, either the standard bar weighing
some twenty-odd pounds or, possibly, in the three and three-
quarter ounce '10-Tola' bars which were both more easily
transported and more readily concealed, say beneath a compressor. For surely it was odd to take back the compressor
in the car when it was already in a boat about to return to
England? In whatever form, however, the gold had been, the
brothers would certainly have quickly got rid of it to a pre-
viously established market. There were, for instance, a large
number of Asians in Britain to whom gold was the irresist-
ible investment, and the 'Tola' a familiar weight. As for the
proceeds, the Strongitharms were unquestionably smart
enough to have evolved some way of evading the law and the
tax inspector.

It was, of course, his duty to report any evidence that gold
had been salvaged and smuggled out of the country. But
what evidence was there? Suspicions based on hearsay and

totally without proof were not welcomed by authority. He picked up a flat stone and sent it spinning out to sea, automatically counting the number of times it touched the surface and leaped onwards before finally sinking. Thirteen.

What was more immediately important was that here was a possible motive for murder. The Pooles had been out in their boat when Perce and Jack made their last diving expedition to Cap Tabal. Could they have seen enough to alarm the brothers? Were the latter afraid that Clarice or Eldred would gossip about what they had seen, or that Eldred might consider it his duty as a model citizen to report it to the authorities? Why, then, had they not immediately disposed of the Pooles? Perhaps because they were within sight of a passing vessel; perhaps because one of the brothers was diving at the time. Had they then awaited the Pooles' return, stopped their boat, drowned them and then disposed of the sole witness, James? The empty fuel tank could be a false clue to what had happened. There might well have been sufficient fuel to take the Pooles to Cala Felix—and the tank could have been emptied to set up a misleading picture.

He moved on, unconscious of the outside world, unresponsive to Shadow's prancing request to be allowed to scamper off on some canine mission. He did not see her fall further and still further behind and then, with a backward glance, race away. His thoughts turned to what Basil had said about the effects of what might be a double intestacy. This was a subject about which the layman would know little or nothing—unless he had purposefully made himself acquainted with it. Bill Eddow seemed an improbable person to have acquired such information. He was unlikely to have been aware that, when the Pooles left England, neither of them had yet made a will. Furthermore, when he learned from Beryl that wills had been made on the eve of death, would he have so quickly disclosed his relationship to the dead man and have asked whether he were a legatee unless he had a clear conscience? Boldness was often the best bluff; but, unless Bill had an unsuspected acting ability, he could not have so convincingly carried out the part of a nervous inquirer. The fact, however, remained, as the Inspector now knew, that Bill had lied about his actions on Monday.

Had Colin, too, lied? He had known his uncle and aunt well, and it was not improbable that, when he last saw them in England, he had been aware that neither had made a will. He could, however, scarcely have known of the wills made and witnessed last Sunday, or of the intended codicil. If he, like everyone else, thought Clarice to be younger than her husband, he had reason to assume himself to be a beneficiary if she died intestate. Until Bill had declared his relationship, he could also assume, provided that he had the necessary legal knowledge, that Eldred's estate would in like manner come to him through his aunt. Provided he had the necessary legal knowledge, the Inspector repeated to himself. As for opportunity, there were no witnesses to the alibi he had given. But had he need of an alibi? He could not possibly have known that the Pooles would be by the inlet to La Caleta between say half past one and half past two. Suppose, however, that he had been on the hillside above the bay when the boat reached the inlet, had recognized the occupants, had seen whatever occurred when the boat upset and had seized the unexpected opportunity to dispose of them and of the solitary witness, James, who would also have seen the Pooles in trouble and have gone to their assistance. Then, the deed done, Colin had waited until someone arrived to find him desperately and vainly attempting to revive a corpse.

Yet, it was difficult to imagine Colin as a triple murderer, as a young man so greedy for money that there was little he would not do to acquire it. The Inspector sighed. No one can tell where the seeds of murder will find fertile soil. To the rest of the world a psychotic may seem as normal as themselves. It is not until the volcano blows that the engulfing lava emerges.

"Hello." Thersie lay on a flat rock, her long tanned legs blending into the cinnamon-coloured stone. She sat up to make room for him. "Perce and Jack are mending something that went wrong with my car, and Colin's helping them. They're having a lovely time getting smothered in grease, so I thought I'd leave them to it."

He sat down, and for some moments they remained in companionable silence. The sun was now low and the sky softening with the first indications of dusk. Pin-points of silver flashed like flying-fish on a frolic sea.

"Were you thinking about Colin?" the Inspector asked. His voice held no curiosity, only the sympathetic interest of friend talking to friend.

"Yes, I was." She looked into the distance, chin cupped in hand. "I'm worried. If I tell you why, will you answer me truly?"

"As truly as I can," he promised.

"He had a telegram this afternoon from the bank. They know nothing about his uncle and aunt's wills, nor who their solicitors are. Colin showed the wire to Basil, told him about the burned will and the unfinished one and asked if Basil could advise him what to do next. Basil explained the position in law. When Colin told me this and that you'd had a talk with him this afternoon I didn't say anything, but I've been thinking about it ever since. He said his aunt would leave quite a lot of money—and I wondered whether anyone," she kept her face averted, "whether anyone who didn't know him as well as I do could imagine that he had anything to do with her death. You see, I realize that he can't actually prove where he was when she drowned." With a rush she went on, "I *know* he couldn't do anything wrong, but I wasn't certain whether you did."

She's young and innocent and in love, the Inspector said to himself, and she knows him little better than I do. She doesn't appreciate that a teacher of sociology must have some acquaintance with the law, certainly enough to know where to find what information he might have sought.

"Anyone who was or could have been near La Caleta at the time is a possible suspect," he said. "But that doesn't mean that Colin is any more under suspicion than Perce or Jack or Juan. I have no evidence to support any supposition that Colin has not told me the truth." He met her gaze. "Does that make you feel better?"

"Much better." Hesitantly she went on, "I know I shouldn't be talking to you like this. You probably think I'm interfering."

"And aren't you?" he asked with a smile.

"Of course I am," she agreed. "But I don't have to tell Colin that I've talked to you about him."

"You don't think that he himself may be worrying?"

"He said he wasn't, and I don't think he is. He's the kind of man who's always looking forward to the future, to the next challenge. Anyone who wants to follow him will have to move fast, but," her face suddenly sparkled, "I've got long legs. I wonder if they've finished mending the car."

No statement of her wish could have been clearer. The Inspector rose and, taking her hand, pulled her to her feet. "I think you were in the bar," he said, "when Mrs Poole mentioned seeing one of the bank robbers."

Thersie nodded. "Yes, I remember how excited she was."

"Do you remember who suggested that the police should be told what she'd seen?"

"Basil did, but she didn't want to. And Eldred said there was nothing she could tell them that would be of any use."

"And what did the others say?"

She smiled. "Perce, or it may have been Jack, advised her to keep her mouth shut. I don't remember anyone else saying anything. She and Eldred left almost at once, and I followed them out. That's when I heard them talking about her will. And," her voice saddened, "that was the last time I saw James—or, rather, heard him. I went down to the beach and was sitting there thinking when he and Gregory walked past behind me. I think they were discussing something on which they were going to work together." She repeated what James had said. "I didn't catch Gregory's answer, but I remember James saying something about letting the Lord decide. He sounded terribly tired. They walked on, and I got up and went to bed. And that was when I found that I'd left the door key inside the bungalow and was locked out. I was trying one of the windows when Perce and Jack turned up, and Perce managed somehow to open the door." She raised her arm and waved. "Oh, there's Colin."

The Inspector watched them meet. If Colin's face were any guide to his feelings, Thersie would not have to exercise her long legs.

The Bar Felix was empty except for Enrique standing in apparently deep thought behind the counter, and Miss Clegg, a glass of gin and tonic at her elbow, looking at yesterday's issue of the *Daily Record*. She beckoned the Inspector with sisterly imperiousness and handed him the newspaper. "Tell me what you think about this," she said briskly. "I won't say a word until you've finished."

Obediently the Inspector began to read.

Under the headline "A Modern Robin Hood Points Out YOUR Crime" the newspaper's Special Crime Reporter described in somewhat highly coloured prose the receipt of a small, square box enclosed in an envelope the reverse side of which bore the name of White's Temperance Hotel, Sheffield. The postmark was London, E.C.1. His own name and the address of the newspaper had been strip-printed by a labelling machine. He opened the box to find a recording tape. Across the hub of the reel a strip of adhesive ribbon carried the typed message 'Please play immediately.' Curious, but suspecting that a colleague had prepared some sort of elaborate leg-pull, he put the tape into his machine and turned the switch.

"This is what I heard," he wrote. "You may believe it, or you may not. I personally think that it has the ring of complete truth. Even if it is true in part only, it puts us, every single one of us, face to face with a problem which we have been sweeping under the carpet for generations, a problem which has been increasing day by day, hour by hour, and which, unless it is tackled quickly and efficiently at the highest levels, will shortly turn every prison cell into a breeding-place of crime and every prisoner into a menace beyond redemption. Well, let the man who recorded this tape speak to you, to all of us. As I write, his voice is in my ears, a disguised voice in all probability, but nevertheless a sincere and compelling one. Listen.

" 'I am a bank robber (the tape begins). I and three friends who think as I do have during the past five years robbed the following banks.' (Here the speaker gives a list of twelve banks. This list has been checked with Scotland Yard, at whose request the names and addresses are being withheld.) 'The robberies have been carried out with the minimum of force. No one has been injured; no one has had to endure more than temporary inconvenience.

" 'From the twelve banks we have taken a total of a little over one hundred thousand pounds. We have spent most of it, but not on ourselves. The money has been spent on discharged prisoners, on men and women who have blundered and been found out, sentenced and put into gaol. Their mistakes have been committed in stupidity, in desperate need, in sudden anger, or because they have been persuaded by others to do something against their nature. They are otherwise as good citizens as the majority of us—and better than many.

'With the funds at our disposal—the stolen funds—we have been able to help these people to resume their lives, to support their families, to become normal, honourable, yes honourable, citizens. Without that help fifty per cent of them, perhaps more, would have existed in misery and poverty —and, at last, in desperation, because there was no one willing to help, they would have come to petty pilfering, to another sentence, then to crime, once again to prison, and continued so until they died.

'Whether you like to acknowledge it or not, discharged prisoners are the untouchables of our society. The Aid Societies, the Probation Officers and the Central After-Care Association do what they can, but they can help only a small proportion. What do *you* do—or *you*—or *you*? In most cases, nothing. What does the State do? As little as it can. And why does it do so little? Because it knows that *you* don't want it to do more.

'Let me touch on another side of the matter, the mercenary side—for that is what many of us understand best. Every crime costs money, every robbery has to be paid for by someone. And who pays? You do. In everything that you buy, in every service that you require, the price includes the cost of protection against theft, against lawlessness—and that cost runs into many millions of pounds. Yet you would pay out these millions from your own pockets rather than give a little to help the man who has lapsed so that he will not lapse again.

'I have told you what my friends and I have done, not because we are proud of it, but because I want you to think —and think again—about the future of your country, and to act before the situation becomes irremediable. What can you do? As individuals you can offer understanding and practical help to those who come out of prison into an unwelcoming world. As members of the community, as electors, you have the power, through your Parliamentary representatives, to persuade the Government to devote as much attention to the after-care of those who have paid for their mistakes as they do to bills about blood-sports or to complaints from Members who fancy that their dignity has been injured.

'I have now only this to say. My friends and I have retired from our part-time occupation of bank robbery. It was not one that we enjoyed, though' (here one detects a slight smile in the voice) 'it had its moments of excitement. I am now asking you to do what you can to redeem the blindness and stupidity of the past.'

"Here," wrote the Crime Reporter, "the tape ends. While crime must not be condoned, it is difficult completely to condemn the deeds of this man and his friends, criminals though they may be in the eyes of the law. They have risked their reputations and their freedom to give us a lead. Today the *Daily Record* has opened a Trust Fund and paid into it a cheque for ten thousand pounds. The purpose of this fund is two-fold: to help the ex-prisoner to resume his or her place as a useful and respected citizen, and to induce the Government to bring in the necessary measures to the same end. Smug words and boasts about a Welfare State ring hollow when a sinner is to a great extent excluded from its benefits."

The Inspector glanced through two further paragraphs that dealt with the trusteeship of what the *Daily Record* had christened the 'Conscience Fund' and with the various ways in which contributions could be made, then put down the paper. Miss Clegg waited for him to speak.

"If you are asking me to speak as a policeman," he said with the shadow of a smile, "I have to say that black and white cannot make white. You cannot expect a policeman to say that he approves the breaking of the law, whatever the purpose. But if you want the opinion of a friend who as a boy has often stolen oranges from his neighbours' trees —" He became aware that they were no longer alone and, turning, saw Basil and Antonia behind him, and Gregory, Bill and the Strongitharm brothers in the doorway. "I didn't realize that we had an audience," he said mildly.

"I wasn't eavesdropping intentionally." Gregory moved forward. "I read the story over lunch and passed the paper on to Basil as I'd heard that he was interested in the problems of rehabilitation."

"Jack and me's read it too," said Perce. "Seems to us that if a bloke has the guts to kick the law up the backside to get things moving he's earned hisself a medal. We've had pals what's been inside, and when they've come out we've given them a hand where we could. But I'll tell you this, that most times when it comes to them finding a job you'd think from the way that they was treated that they was flying the yellow flag and had fever, plague, leprosy, the lot. So we takes off our hats to this bloke. If ever I meets him the drinks is on me." He passed his tongue over his lips, and, catching Enrique's eye, gestured pouring out from a glass.

"Let's hear from you, Basil." Miss Clegg's tone brooked no refusal.

"Never ask a lawyer for an opinion off the cuff unless you're prepared for him to hedge." Basil smiled as he stubbed out his cigarette. "But, if you promise not to pass it on to the Law Society, I'll tell you what I feel about this. It takes a bombshell of this kind to bring people to awareness of the facts. As an individual I approve this particular bomb-

133

shell. What Perce said is all too true. Too many ex-prisoners are regarded as lepers; and there can be no question that the present provision for after-care and aid is sadly insufficient. I'd like to add one or two things. One is that the facilities for teaching a man a trade in prison are inadequate, and the miserly pay discourages him from working his best. This can to some extent be blamed on the trade unions who cavil at prison competition. Another point is, of course, what the speaker implied without naming it—the appalling overcrowding and conditions of prison life. The overcrowding is in part due to the imposition of prison sentences when a lesser punishment would serve the purpose better. It is inexcusably wrong that sentences should differ according to who is sitting on the Bench. What is needed is more training of judges and magistrates in this part of their job. All these things are not, of course, the purpose of this Conscience Fund, but they are ancillary to it. But they've been discussed for many years without very much result. What the man who made this tape has done is to select a subject—one might call it the problem of the pariah—which, projected as a bogey, may well shock the country into action. I hope the Fund achieves its object —and I very much hope that this man and his friends remain undiscovered." He grinned. "I've told you my feelings as a private person. As a lawyer I must uphold the law as it stands."

"An idealist on a bearing rein," Gregory commented.

"A man of sense and sensibility," Miss Clegg nodded approvingly. "We understand the reasons for people's actions a great deal better than we did not so many years ago and, while we must still let the law decide the penalty, few of us are now convinced that harsh punishment is in itself a deterrent. Would anyone here agree with the eighteenth-century judge who said to a prisoner, 'You are here to be hanged not because you have stolen a sheep, but in order that others may not steal sheep'?" She looked round the listening faces and added in a voice whose sudden lowering emphasized the words, "Except in the case of murder."

She's been leading up to this, the Inspector said to himself. She chose a time when people come here for a drink before dinner to throw the word 'murder' at them. Does she know or guess something that she hasn't told me? Or did she wish to observe their reactions—and that I should observe them too? Did the fact that Colin was not present have any meaning?

"For heaven's sake can't we keep off the subject of murder?" Bill's tone held petulance. "Can't we try to forget for a moment what happened? I know there's been a lot of gossip and rumour flying around, but isn't it common sense to accept that the probability is that it was just a horrible accident?"

"I think we *should* talk about it," Basil said with decision. "It's no use trying to bottle up what must be in everyone's mind. All of us, or, at any rate, most of us," he added with a shrug, "will be thankful to know the facts."

"All of us, I hope," Gregory responded lightly. "I can't see Bill here as a murderer, or any of you for that matter, and I hope the same goes for me. We don't know, of course, what reasons the Inspector may have for considering the possibility of murder, but I daresay he'd be as happy as the rest of us if he were able to establish that it was an accident."

"I'd be more than happy," the Inspector agreed.

Basil looked sharply up. "But you think it's improbable?"

"I'm always ready to be convinced." He paused; it was a calculated pause which no one was inclined to interrupt. "Perhaps the person who was in La Caleta at the time of James Rowley's death could convince me." In the silence that followed he waited for their response, his face impassive, the violet eyes apparently contemplating the bottles ranged behind the bar.

Miss Clegg's expression was one of unsurprised interest. Juan, who had appeared a minute earlier behind the bar, picked up a cloth and began to polish a glass. Bill rubbed hand against hand as if he were holding them over a basin. Antonia twisted her wedding-ring. Basil's nod and Gregory's 'H'm' implied only that both had been given food for thought. Out of the corner of his mouth Perce whispered to his brother.

Quietly the Inspector rose and left the bar. They would talk more freely if he were not there. Someone might say something that would spark a train of memory in another.

As he strolled towards the hotel, Shadow rejoined him. A warily cocked eye reassured her that he was not going to reprimand her. Sedately she followed, waiting patiently at his side when he stopped to light a cigarette, then to stand in contemplation.

Dusk had now turned to a luminous darkness. Beneath the lamps on the hotel terrace four substantial forms reclined. There were lights in the Pooles' bungalow. Behind him, as he looked out to sea, male crickets shrilled their mating call. If it were true, he thought, that a single cricket could be heard at a distance of half a mile, then either there was a permanent shortage of eligible females, or the incessant, piercing noise served to deter rather than to attract. This was one form of life in which the male out-talked the female.

A figure was momentarily silhouetted against the light from the bar, and Bill came out. His stride seemed to falter as he observed the Inspector and he changed course to pass a few yards away. The Inspector moved to meet him. "I would like to talk to you again about what you did last Monday," he said mildly. "I was interested to hear that you were acquainted with *Señor* Rojais."

"Rojais." Bill shook his head. "I don't know anyone of that name." He spoke with the certainty of someone telling the truth.

"He was the man you met at a café in Palamós."

"That man! How could you possibly know—?" The confidence of a moment ago sank like a soufflé delayed between oven and table. "I—I did talk to a man who shared my table, but I have no idea who he was. I'd never seen him before."

"Why did you tell me that the café you visited was at Calella?"

Indecision fluttered the muscles of the easy-going face.

"Because my going to Palamós had nothing to do with your inquiries. It was my own private business."

"Then you must tell me what that business was." Severity, the Inspector judged, would quickly crumble this man's defense. "You must account for every minute of the time you were out in the launch. You must provide details which can be checked. *Señor* Rojais will no doubt remember the time of your meeting and the subject of your conversation. I need not emphasize that this is a serious matter. The inquiry concerns the deaths of your half-brother and his wife, by which you may well benefit."

"I haven't benefited," Bill said ruefully. "You know that as well as I do."

This sounds like the voice of innocence, the Inspector said to himself, but his tone remained implacable. "Please tell me what you actually did on Monday."

Haltingly Bill began. He had been approached on Sunday by a stranger who asked him if he were willing to accept a fee of fifteen pounds for a simple little job. What was the job? Bill had inquired doubtfully. Smilingly the stranger explained that it was to bring in a few 'blue' films to amuse some of his friends; he would have done the job himself if he had not to be in Madrid on urgent business. All Bill had to do was to pick up a plastic ball which would be thrown overboard from a freighter, take it to a café and hand it to a man who would ask to exchange his matchbox for a box that Bill would carry. The fee would be in the box that Bill received. "It sounded just a bit of fun," Bill excused himself, looking anxiously at the Inspector whose face showed nothing but polite interest. "After all, if a few old boys want to look at a 'blue' film, it doesn't do anyone any harm. You can see them all over London if you want to. And I could do with the money. They don't pay much for the job I'm doing here."

"So you handed over the plastic ball in exchange for the matchbox. Did you open the ball to look at the contents?"

"I did think about it," Bill acknowledged frankly. "But it was sealed watertight."

"So you don't know what you actually brought ashore?"

"N-no, I suppose not." Under the steady gaze of the violet eyes Bill fidgeted uncomfortably.

"I see." The Inspector fell silent, considering the worried face, the awkward stance of a schoolboy caught out in some wrongdoing, the nervous half-clenching of the hands. It sounds like part of a spy story for children, he was thinking, and because it is so childish it is believable. "You have admitted to smuggling," he said evenly. "You will understand that I cannot keep this information to myself. Further inquiries will have to be made, and you may well find that you have to repeat to others what you have told me. I cannot say what action will be taken in your case. If you have told me the whole truth, that will no doubt be taken into consideration."

"I've told you everything," Bill said hoarsely.

"Were you planning to return to England with your party?"

"No, my job's finished when I've seen them onto the 'plane."

"What did you intend to do then?"

"Carmen said she'd put me up for a few days. Then I suppose I'll go back to England and find something to do in the winter."

There are so many of his kind who come to Spain, the Inspector reflected; unqualified, basically idle men who take a job in the sunshine that leads nowhere. They try to make a little money on the side, and nine times out of ten get into trouble with their employers or with the law. They are today's Micawbers, aimlessly awaiting what will never turn up. One could not dislike Bill; one should not condemn him for being as he was born. But, until his story was confirmed, he must remain on the list of possible suspects. In the Inspector's mind was the thought that, if the facts as known and Basil's interpretation of them were correct, Bill would find himself Eldred's heir, and his financial troubles at least would be solved.

"Do you happen to know what your half-brother's age was?" he asked.

"Fifty-two or thereabouts, I think."

"And his wife's?"

"I couldn't say." A short pause. "Four or five years younger, I'd guess. Colin will probably know."

The Inspector bade him good night and watched his progress to the hotel. Gradually Bill's gait assumed a sort of jauntiness. Over the evening air, a little off key, came the sound of a whistled song. Was it the expression of a man trying to keep up his courage—or could it be that of one who has made a false confession and is convinced that he has been believed?

In a short while the Inspector went to his car, parked by the side of the hotel. From the darkness Shadow leaped to his side. Driving slowly and pensively to the Cuartel in Pala-frugell, he made several telephone calls; to the *Teniente* at Palamós, to the Harbour Master at Mataró, and to Marseilles.

Then he rang his home.

"Oh, darling." Benita's voice sparkled over the line. "I was hoping you'd ring."

"Is there anything wrong?" he asked anxiously.

"I'm bouncing with health—and so's the baby. But I've done it again—I don't have to tell you what."

He laughed. "You've got the sink stopped up."

"Yes—and I can't find that rubber plunger thing. It's not in its place under the sink."

"Look in the bathroom, below the basin. You used it there on Wednesday."

"Oh, so I did. I thought I might need it again there. My brain goes all fuzzy when you're away," she said disconsolately. "When d'you think you'll be back?"

"I don't know. I'm trying to unravel the knots from the usual bundle of lies. I'll call you again very soon."

"Don't hang up," she said quickly. "Your mother rang yesterday. She's going to give us a pram or a cot, and she wants to know which we'd like."

"Did you gather whether she herself had any preference?"

"She mentioned a cot that she'd seen and nearly bought."

"Then there's no problem, is there, darling?"

"You mean that a dutiful wife will accept what her mother-in-law decides?" There was a smile in her voice.

"In matters like that, yes. She'll have given us something she herself has chosen, and we'll have got something we need. Give her my love when you ring—and add a little judicious flattery about her choice."

It was as he drove back to Cala Felix that there suddenly came into his mind some words that Benita had spoken. Earlier that evening Miss Clegg had made a comment in which similar words occurred. Momentarily his hands tightened on the steering-wheel as he realized that a remark made last Sunday, and casually repeated to him, might have been misinterpreted. He recalled, not for the first time, what someone had once said, that a detective was a prophet looking backwards.

11

Friday morning and afternoon, 15ᵗʰ September

Shortly after seven o'clock the Inspector came out onto the balcony of his room. The rising sun streaked the sky with alternate layers of pastel pink and blue, a candy-striped sheet paled by many washings. Absently he fiddled with the ring on the little finger of his right hand, revealing a circle of paler skin. Suddenly he recalled the mercurochrome on Basil's hand when he first saw him at the petrol station. He clicked finger against thumb.

Was it beyond possibility that Basil had been one of the bank robbers, the leader, the man who had recorded the tape? He had been in England at the time—and so had Antonia, who might well have been the 'boy' among the party of four. Resting his hands on the rail, the Inspector concentrated. Miss Clegg had mentioned Basil's work for the ex-prisoners whom he called his 'untouchables'. The same word had been used in that context on the tape. What, he asked himself, did he really know about Basil, about the man behind the friendly facade? He had no illusions about his ability to judge character on short acquaintance. Too often in the past he had been mistaken. Even a lifetime of friendship was insufficient for judgment. The racing motorist one has thought fearless may draw back with a shiver from the edge of a precipice, the parachutist of many hundred jumps may shy at the sight of a slow-worm, but these weaknesses re-

141

main unknown until circumstances reveal them. It was possible that Basil had put mercurochrome on his hand—and on two fingers for more convincing effect—to conceal the telltale white circle of skin beneath a ring that had been quickly removed when Clarice mentioned the signet ring worn by the man leaving the bank by the side door.

Basil, others had said, was an idealist; and the idealist who is strong-willed and fanatical balks at little to achieve his purpose. He will sacrifice himself; he may also not hesitate to sacrifice others so that he remains free to conceal or continue that purpose. Basil had lived a life of danger during the war, a life in which he could neither expect nor show mercy, in which the elimination of a possible informer was essential for his own safety. Had, then, Clarice died because she had seen Basil coming out of the bank—and the two witnesses of her death then been disposed of? It was conceivable; but was it likely? Certainly Basil knew that the Pooles were going out in the boat. He could have known that they intended to return for lunch, waited and swum out to meet them. The Inspector sighed. He would have to go still more closely into the times of Basil's visit to Mataró.

The putt-putt of an engine in some unseen fishing boat broke his train of thought. The brightening sun was dispersing a thin morning haze over the bay where Juan's boats lay almost motionless at their moorings. Nearby on the beach a heap of sand was all that remained of the castle which Bill had painstakingly helped Carmen's children to build. Further to the left, Gregory, towel slung over shoulder, was pausing outside Basil's bungalow to light a cigarette. His tightly clinging beach shorts indicated that he had already swum. As if conscious of a watcher, he glanced at the balcony and raised an arm in greeting.

While he lathered his face the Inspector returned to his earlier thoughts. It was not difficult to build a card house if one had a firm base on which to start construction; but to build a case against a possible suspect on one's own personal interpretation of hearsay was as foolish as to try to shave with a razor into which one has not inserted a blade. And this, he realized, as he unscrewed the razor, was exactly what he had been doing. Taking a blade from its wrapping, he dropped it into place. The gears of his brain, he reflected, were not in mesh. A walk before breakfast might re-engage them. He had scarcely completed dressing before Shadow's instinctive reading of her master's thoughts had taken her into the bedroom to stand expectantly before the door.

As he left the hotel he saw in the distance Enrique trundling the ancient trolley into which he tipped the rubbish buckets that each household put out at night. Reaching the banjo and circling the Pooles' house, he turned onto the footpath that ran behind the houses and led, across the dirt road, to a cluster of pine-trees at the back of the hotel and to the communal rubbish dump. Branches of spurge and cistus growing over the little-used path brushed against his trousers, and prickly oak and spined wild asparagus scratched at his ankles.

A rustle in the undergrowth, and Shadow was no longer at his heel. For a few seconds her leaping progress was audible, then there was silence. On the other side of the dirt road the track became wider and showed signs of regular use. It was there that Shadow rejoined him, an oak-leaf clinging to her top-knot, an eye cocked to receive a welcome. They reached the rubbish dump to find Enrique tipping out the last of the buckets from the trolley. An exchange of weather lore followed the morning greetings, and a few minutes passed before the barman, prophesying rain before the next day, wheeled the trolley away.

Already flies and a large white butterfly were prospecting among the newly added litter, in which were various items whose recent owners were almost certainly identifiable. Nine or ten India Pale Ale cans and one labelled 'Tripe and Onions' could be attributed to the Strongitharm brothers; a sandal with a broken strap was one of a pair that he had seen Thersie wearing; the brand name on a light-blue tin was that of the tobacco which Brian smoked. Shadow sniffed at a partly open paper bag and, with a watchful eye on her master, scraped at it with a paw. The paper parted to disclose a well-used emery board, some lipsticked tissues, a flattened tube that had contained shaving-cream and two small bottles, an empty one labelled 'Seconal', the other holding the hardened residue of a nail varnish recognizable as that used by Antonia.

Was Antonia taking a hypnotic? A young woman who simply sparkled with health, whose days were being spent in sea and sunshine, who to outward appearances was with the man she loved, would surely not require an aid to sleep. Could it be Basil who was suffering from insomnia? Or could this be the bottle he had seen among the medicines ranged on the shelves in James's bathroom? If so, how had it now reached the rubbish tip? Picking it up, he put it in his pocket and returned to the hotel. It was the sight of Millie talking to Miss Clegg at the breakfast table that turned his thoughts into another channel. As he drank his coffee he was recalling her artless confession.

Gregory caught up with him as he reached his bedroom door. There was a half-smile on his lips and a twinkle in the light-blue eyes. "Millie's told me that she's spilled the beans," he said. "Look, come into my room for a moment. It's rather more private than the passage." He opened the door and waited for the Inspector to precede him.

The maids had been in the room while Gregory breakfasted. The bedspread, tucked under and then taken over the twin pillows in the Spanish fashion, was unwrinkled. On the doorward side of the bed a low table held a travelling clock and a carafe of water covered by an inverted glass. On the other side a shelf held a Concise Oxford Dictionary, a Thesaurus, half a dozen jacketed copies of *No End of a World* and a pile of paperbacks. Within arm's-reach of the shelf and beside the open French windows leading to the balcony stood a large, sturdy table on which were a covered portable typewriter flanked by several folders, an exercise book, a ball-point pen, two pencils, an ashtray and a packet of cigarettes. The exercise book lay open at a page half-filled with notes in a neat, angular hand.

"I'm sorry I had to spin you a yarn," Gregory said, "But

144

I'm sure you understand—"

"That you were protecting a lady's reputation," the Inspector completed the sentence.

Gregory nodded solemnly. "I know you'd have done the same. What else could one do?" He was speaking as man to man, and there was a tinge of masculine self-satisfaction in his voice. "But, if you had to find out, I'm glad it wasn't through me—though, for the life of me, I can't think how you got it out of Millie."

"She told me in order to protect you."

"To protect me?" Gregory exclaimed in surprise; then a look of comprehension came into his face. "Oh, I see. You mean she was giving me an alibi for the time those poor devils drowned." He gazed soberly at the other man. "Poor kid, I suppose you had to ask her. Of course, everyone who was here that day would be on your list of suspects." He moved over to the table, picked up the packet of cigarettes, held it out and, when the Inspector declined, lit one for himself and puffed thoughtfully. "Well, if Millie's told you everything, there doesn't seem much for me to say except that she's an even nicer kid than I thought. It must have been damned embarrassing for her."

The Inspector made a gesture of assent. He was looking in the direction of the bedside shelf, and from the movement of his eyes might have been counting the number of books. "I mustn't keep you from your work," he said.

"Any excuse not to get down to work is a good one to a writer," Gregory smiled. "In any case, there was something I wanted to ask you. You said last night, or rather you implied it, that someone was with James in La Caleta last Monday. Naturally we discussed this when you left. Since all of us knew we were not there at the time, we could only conclude that you were speaking of some outsider. But what had us stuck was to think of some explanation as to how an outsider could possibly have known where any of those three unfortunates would be that day. We decided that he couldn't have known and that therefore he must have been there by chance—and that, if he were there by chance, it's extremely unlikely that he had anything to do with the drownings unless he were a maniac of some sort—a psychopath or what-have-you. Does that seem reasonable to you?"

"Eminently reasonable," the Inspector agreed, "granting your premisses."

"Granting—?" Gregory looked puzzled, then smiled. "But we must all have known where we were unless we were mental cases or suffering from amnesia, surely? I think it was Carmen who suggested what we all felt must be the answer. It's the kind of thing that's often happened before, and I suppose it will go on happening. A stranger is on the beach and watches it all happen. Either he's an indifferent swimmer and feels he can't help, or he's frightened of risking his own life. He goes away and keeps silence because he knows that if he says he was there he'll be branded at the least as a coward. As I said, that kind of thing's not so uncommon. Isn't it more likely than that someone killed three harmless people?"

"Perhaps." The inflection of the Inspector's voice was encouraging.

"Good lord, what reason could anyone have had to wish any of them dead?" Gregory stubbed out his cigarette. "The Pooles seemed a pretty inoffensive couple, and no one could wish to do James any harm. Look at Basil, Colin, Perce, Jack, the rest of them. Can you see any of them as a killer? Come to that, haven't they all got perfectly good alibis?"

"An alibi requires at least one reliable witness. You, for instance, can speak for Millie just as she has spoken for you. In some other cases the alibis are at present less than complete." The Inspector moved towards the door. "In my experience, Mr Warrack, the perfect alibi usually depends on circumstances to which the person concerned has given little prior thought."

Looking at the closing door, Gregory rubbed his cheek. The implications of the Inspector's final remark were clear —but whom could he have in mind?

Half an hour later the Inspector blew water from his nose,

turned on his back and floated. Out of the corner of an eye he could see the point of Cap Rubí. He must, he reckoned, be about two hundred metres from the beach. Why, he asked himself, had no one invented an instrument like a pedometer to measure the distance one had swum? Perhaps someone had done so and found no buyers. Perhaps somewhere in some dark cellar several thousand small boxes were piled high, each containing a tissue-wrapped 'Swimometer', seen only by nibbling mice and rejected as inedible. Yet there were apparently ready buyers for many things of even less practical use: combined shoe-horns and bottle-openers, curved scissors for cutting the tops from eggs, mink-trimmed hot-water bottle covers, hand-painted chopping boards—the list was unending. But enough of such idle considerations. He was at Cala Felix to establish whether or not murder had been committed and, if murder could be proved, to find the murderer. And to collect and collate his thoughts he had betaken himself to the sea, to the element which he had found on more than one occasion to be a fruitful thinking-mattress.

In the absence of clear evidence it was inevitable that one should theorize. But the danger of theorizing was that one tended to make such facts as had emerged fit a theory. Then objectivity dulled and, whatever new facts came to light, one found oneself incapable of discarding that theory—like the aborigine who was given a new boomerang and tried in vain to throw the old one away.

A movement caught his eye. Inshore a powerful crawl stroke was taking a white-capped head across the bay. As the swimmer reached a rock and clambered onto it, he recognized Miss Clegg. He watched her dive and make, with unexpected speed and style, for the shore; he then resumed his thoughts. They were about rubbish or, to be more exact, about what he had observed earlier on the rubbish tip. Searching his memory, he recalled a brief conversation with Beryl. A line of speculation began to form in his mind.

Noisily, near at hand, someone spat water, and he turned his head. A few metres away Perce was coming towards him, a look of determination on the crook-nosed face. A splash from the opposite direction—and there was Jack, his teeth bared in an anticipatory grin. Was it mischief that lit his countenance, nothing more than mischief? Instinctively the Inspector rolled over and, jack-knifing, dived before either could reach him. Thirty seconds later he came to the surface, drew breath and struck out for the shore. This, he said to himself, will have to be my record time for the two hundred metres. Gasping, he swallowed a little water. Was it imagination, the feeling that someone had grasped at his foot? At long last, reaching the shelving margin of the bay, he staggered out to stumble over a dancing, barking Shadow and to fall at the feet of an astonished Miss Clegg. After him, to collapse panting on the other side, came Perce and Jack.

"Are you three training for the Olympics?" Miss Clegg enquired curiously.

No one had breath to reply. Moments passed before Perce cleared his throat and, ejecting a mouthful of water, sat up. "By gum," he said hoarsely, "you swim like a bloody otter. We could do with you in our team back home. Jack's our champ, but I reckon you could give him a couple of yards." He coughed, then chuckled. "Thought we'd caught you napping, but you must have got eyes in the back of your head."

The Inspector made an inarticulate sound. A thin brown foot by his head moved sideways, and he heard Miss Clegg's voice on a note of angry astonishment. "Do you mean to say you were going to duck him? You were, weren't you? Well, just listen to me, you pair of half-witted schoolboys. Don't you know better than to push someone suddenly under water. If you were in my class I'd take out the cane and give you both a good larruping. Bone-heads, that's what you are. Mutton-heads. Idiots. Imbeciles. Oafs."

"We wouldn't have done him no harm," Jack said placatingly. "We just meant to have a bit of fun."

"Fun." Her tone would have withered a field of barley. "You might have drowned him. A couple of experienced divers like you—and you do a thing like that. You ought to be certified. Get up at once and apologize to the Inspector, or I'll never speak to you again."

"Sorry," they muttered in dutiful unison; then Perce went on admiringly, "Ain't had such a tongue-lashing in years, not even from the missus. School where our kids is could do with someone like you." He drew a deep breath. "Now we've got it over, there ain't no ill-feeling anywhere, is there?" He glanced anxiously at the Inspector and received a reassuring shake of the head—and was that a flicker of the eyelid? "Tell you what. Let's go and have something to take the salt out of our throats. A couple of bottles of beer should suit us fine."

"They may suit you," said Miss Clegg, "but not me. Nothing less than a bottle of champagne, dry and the very best that Carmen can give us," she continued inexorably, "will wash this monstrous episode from my mind."

"About that chap you said was with James in the little bay," said Perce, putting down his glass, "well, I know it needn't have been a chap, but seems to me the chances is it were—did you mean you got evidence there was someone there, or just that there must have been someone if James and the others was murdered?"

The Inspector considered the question and decided to tell them about the towel. They would be in doubt as to how much more he knew. Doubt and suspense were useful weapons in a detective's armoury.

"Pity Colin couldn't remember the colours," Jack commented. "I'd have thought he c'd have seen what they was. Most folk can tell colours apart up to five hundred yards. Must have been more than one colour, I reckon. If it's just one, it sticks in your mind. Only towel around here I can call to mind is that tomato-y one of Thersie's."

Some minutes later the Inspector declined Jack's pressing invitation to come diving from Juan's launch during the afternoon, and walked to the hotel with Miss Clegg. The bottle of champagne which she had consumed unaided seemed in no whit to have affected her. It was not until they were parting that she said with a self-deprecatory chuckle, "I've never yet taken a siesta, but I think I may well fall asleep this afternoon."

After lunch the Inspector took his note-book and thoughts onto the terrace. Shortly the Arkells and Smurthwaites joined him there, to lie back in attitudes of contented repletion. Eyes closed, the ladies dozed. The men, each with catalogue in hand, rumbled away about the merits of some calculating machine which, it appeared, the merest baby, if so inclined, could operate from its cradle. Soon the Inspector, seeking silence, rose and made for the cleft to La Caleta. Passing Gregory's balcony, he glanced upward. Gregory was standing, pencil in hand, staring seawards with the unfocused eyes of deep concentration, a concentration undisturbed by Shadow's yap as a seagull swooped to pass a few feet above her head.

Emerging from the other end of the cleft, the Inspector observed Beryl and Cyril on a rock half way down the far side of the inlet. They were close-clasped, motionless except for the hand with which she was tracing the knobby protuberances of his vertebrae. Millie sat on the sand, knees drawn up to her chin, her attitude signifying loneliness and despondency. Then, like a moth attuned to vibrations that only her kind can sense, she turned her head. Gladness and welcome lit her face and she waved as to somebody whom she could count a friend. It was with a feeling that he was failing her in her need for companionship that, responding with a wave of the hand, he continued on his way to the topmost point of Cap Rubí. There he sat down and, lighting a cigarette, directed his mind to the question of 'How?' For now he had little doubt about 'Who?'

From his point of vantage he could view the little world of his inquiry. Beryl and Cyril were still close-clasped. Millie had turned onto her face and unfastened the clasp of her bikini top. In Cala Felix, Connie and Roddie were digging a moat round a new sandcastle. Side by side Thersie and Colin swam towards the beach down which Basil and Antonia came to meet them. Gregory, now in bathing trunks, towel as usual slung over a shoulder, was talking to Carmen outside the door of James's bungaiow. The sideways cock of his head and the movements of his hands gave an impression that he was using all his charm of persuasion. She shook her head and, locking the door behind her, gave him what looked like a friendly shove and tripped off to the bar. For a moment Gregory stood indecisively before striding onto the beach, throwing down the towel, running into the water and striking out across the bay. He passed within a few yards of the launch where Juan was busying himself. Shortly, Perce and Jack appeared laden with equipment and boarded the launch. Their joshing of one another and of Juan could be heard before the engine started and the boat moved off.

When the Inspector rose it was with the suddenness of a man who has forgotten or omitted to do something. He came down fast from Cap Rubí and, making for the bar, asked Carmen for the key to James's bungalow.

"I've just been along there myself to turn off the fridge," she said. "Forgot about it when we were there together. Greg'll be after you later. He wants to borrow a book of James's about Brazil to check on something he's writing. I said to ask you." Her face crinkled with amusement as she commented, "Miss Clegg didn't half dip her nose in the champagne this morning."

"I think she's probably sleeping it off now." He smiled as he took the key.

Once inside the bungalow he glanced along the bookshelves and, finding a copy of the *South American Handbook for 1969,* took it down and placed it on the desk. His eye was caught by a leather-bound copy of the picaresque romance *Lazarillo de Tormes* which, he noted from the lettering on the spine, had been published in England. Curiosity led him to find out the name of the translator. The book opened at the fly-leaf on which an inscription read, "To James with love from Tommy—Christmas, 1947." His eyebrows rose. The handwriting was one which he had seen not long before. Slowly he closed the book and, picking up the *Handbook* and the two orange folders from the desk, went out onto the terrace and sat down in the shade. Unconscious

151

of all else—of the happy cries of Carmen's children on the sand, of the sound of the returning launch, of glances from Colin, Bill, Escipión and others who passed by—he turned the pages. He had closed the folder and was about to put it down and pick up the other one when a self-amused voice said, "I've had my siesta and enjoyed it. I hope it's not the beginning of a habit. No, I see I'm disturbing you. I shouldn't have spoken." Miss Clegg was moving away when he called to her and, bringing another chair into the shade, asked her to sit down.

"I think you might like to have a book which was on Mr Rowley's shelves," he said.

She glanced at the volume in his hand. "Oh, dear!" The exclamation came with an undertone of sadness. After a pause she asked, "Aren't you going to say anything more?"

"Isn't it for you to say it?" he replied gently.

"Yes, I suppose it is." Her tone was almost brusque. "I gave it to him the Christmas before he married. I should have told you I once knew him."

"And why didn't you tell me?"

She looked directly into his eyes and found only sympathetic interest. "Because no one wants to dig up the past when there's no future to it. Would it have helped you in your inquiries to know that many years ago we had been friends?"

"It would have explained something that has puzzled me—why, when your interest in coming to this part of Spain was antiquity, you chose to stay here and not at, say, La Escala or Torroella de Montgrí. Here there is nothing but sea and sand. There is no public transport. And you are with a group of which only one member has a tiny grain of intellectual curiosity."

She gave an appreciative nod. "Alpha marks, Inspector. You mean that I stick out like a white blackbird. I suppose I do. I'm here because James and I met by chance in London. I'd taken my sister to see a specialist in Harley Street, and James was in the waiting-room when we arrived. It was the first time we'd met since he told me about the girl he was going to marry. We'd been friends for some time before that, for more than two years. I'd hoped he would ask me to marry him, but he didn't. I was a Plain Jane, even plainer than I am now, and I hadn't learned that men shy away from girls who display their knowledge as if it were a jewel in a woman's crown. It may be a jewel, but—" She sighed.

"It should be kept in a ten times barr'd up chest until after marriage," the Inspector said with a smile.

"Richard Two." She turned to face him. "It's easy to talk to you because we're on the same wavelength. But then you're on everybody's wavelength."

"I haven't yet tuned in to the transmission that would close this inquiry," he said wryly.

Neither broke the silence while a lizard scuttered across the tiles in front of them, stopped momentarily to eye coldly the two-legged monsters and scurried away to safety. Miss Clegg watched it disappear, then said abruptly, "I've told you how James and I met again. We had lunch and exchanged life stories. I happened to mention that I was coming out to this part of Spain in September, and he said he had a bungalow here and would be coming out at that time with a car. We could visit ancient monuments together, he suggested—and so on." The clasped hands on her lap tightened. "Well, we met again several times, and I thought things over and changed my booking to a tour that was coming to this hotel—and I was here, as you know, when he arrived. We had a talk late that afternoon. He hadn't told anyone about me—there was no reason why he should. I'd already booked in London for the Ampurias tour since he hadn't expected to arrive here until Monday or Tuesday. Her shoulders moved in what might have been a shrug or a shiver. "That's all."

She had told the story simply and without change of tone, almost as if it had happened to two people with whom she was slightly acquainted. Would he ever know, the Inspector wondered, whether the bud of her youthful affection for James had withered with the years? She seemed to guess his thoughts for, with a suddenness that took him by surprise, she said, "Don't imagine that I was chasing James. If anything, it was the other way round. He felt the need of affection, and I could offer only friendship, and I told him so very plainly. I'm not one of those people who wants to resuscitate their own past. I've made my life what it is, and I'm content with it. To paraphrase the first Queen Elizabeth, 'I count the glory of my crown that I have reigned with the love of children.' " She snorted. "There I go again showing off my knowledge. If you haven't got any more questions I'll take myself off."

"No more questions," the Inspector said gently. He held out the book and she took it; then he watched her stride away until she turned right towards the main road. Soon he picked up the second folder and began to read.

Pura hung up the cloth with which she had wiped down the washing-machine, closed the lid and came into the shop. She was bone-tired, and her heart sank to see so much untidiness and dust. Luis sat sprawled in a chair behind the counter, half asleep, clutching a crumpled newspaper. He opened his eyes at her cluck of irritation.

"What have you done with the things that the *recadero* brought?" she asked.

"He left them by the step outside."

"You might have brought them in," she said wearily. "Come and give me a hand with the crates." She went out, returning with a large carton. "Did he bring the cleaning fluid?"

"He said so." Luis bent forward slowly and picked up a piece of paper from the counter. "It's on his bill."

"Well, it's not outside. Didn't you check what he brought?"

"No, I didn't. I had other things to do," Luis said truculently. "There were people in and out of the shop all the afternoon."

Pura signed. She knew there would have been only one or two customers. "He must have left it in his van. I'll ask Juan if he can pick it up when he goes in tomorrow. Aren't you going to help me with the crates?"

"In a minute," Luis snarled. "I'm tired, woman. Tired of this damned shop—and sick of being nagged. God knows why you had to bring us here."

She spread her hands in a gesture of hopeless despondency. "Yes," she muttered to herself. "God knows."

12

Friday evening,
15th September

CLOSING THE ORANGE folder, the Inspector looked at his watch to find that it was not yet seven o'clock. From the failing light he had judged it to be later. The sky was now obscured by heavy black clouds rolling cumbrously seaward. It seemed that Enrique's prophecy of rain would be fulfilled. A leaden sea stretched as far as the eye could see. There was not a soul on the beach; the silence was almost oppressive. Even the crickets had ceased their clamant shrillness and retired to their shallow tunnels.

Rising, he went indoors and into the bathroom. The rows of bottles he had seen yesterday on the shelves appeared undisturbed. He picked up one. Shortly, dropping a piece of screwed-up tissue paper into a pocket, he locked the bungalow door behind him and, tucking folders and handbook under an arm, made his way to the hotel.

Shadow raced ahead, doubled back and, with a questioning sideways glance, tore past, flying feet leaving a wake of sand. She needs more exercise than I'm giving her, the Inspector said to himself. Let her run herself into contented exhaustion. She can come to no harm here.

He entered the hall to find it deserted; but light shining from the half-open door of Escipión's office intimated that the manager was at work—or, perhaps, snatching a short rest. The passage to his room lay in darkness, and no light came when he pressed and re-pressed the switch. Moving slowly in the dimness, he noted subconsciously that the door of the empty bedroom adjoining his stood ajar. He was bending, key in hand, at his own door when he remembered self-exasparatedly what he had omitted to look for in the bungalow. He must return there at once. As he began to straighten up he became conscious of soft, swift footsteps behind. Before he could turn, a heavy hand chopped brutally at his neck and he slumped forward, book and folders falling to the floor. Firm hands seized him below the arms and propelled him headlong into the linen cupboard. Stumbling, he smacked painfully against a shelf and fell. Metal clanged beside him, the door closed and a key turned in the lock. Then there was silence except for the sound of gurgling liquid and an overpowering odour.

It was as he staggered to his feet that he recognized the smell. Carbon tetrachloride—cleaning fluid. He panted, and his throat seemed to contract. For a moment he stayed leaning against a shelf; then, bending unsteadily, he searched with both hands until he touched metal. Liquid was still gurgling as he lifted the container and, tearing the handkerchief from his breast-pocket, rammed it into the neck.

A lurching step took him to the door to search and search, to find that there was no handle and to remember with unease that the door opened inwards. But it will be, he told himself, like all the doors in the hotel, made only of plywood on a frame. A step backward, and he kicked at the panel. Thoughts raced confusedly through his head as he kicked and kicked again. Surely tetrachloride was not inflammable? He could use his cigarette lighter—but what purpose would a light serve? Breathe through a piece of filtering material? Useless. A spasm gripped his throat. Time passed at tortoise pace while he continued to kick with diminishing force at the unyielding door. Then the sound of frenzied barking and the desperate scrabbling of paws. Another spasm. Suddenly noise reverberated through the cupboard as someone smashed at the lock. A splintering crash followed and the door burst inwards.

Faces bent over him. Basil's. Gregory's. Miss Clegg's. Escipión's. Then he was lying on his own bed. Through pain that shot like forked lightning through his head he saw Basil standing by the open window. Miss Clegg sat beside him, Shadow at her feet, unwinking eyes swivelling anxiously from one to the other. "Get folders dropped in passage," he croaked, and saw Basil hasten out before nausea gripped him and he vomited into the basin that Miss Clegg held.

"Lie still," she said as she lowered his head onto the pillow, and he lay obediently while she passed a damp sponge over his face. When she had dried him he took hold of her restraining hand. "I want you to do something for me at once. In my jacket pocket you'll find the key to James's bungalow. There should be some papers there." Carefully he described what she was to look for. "I think they may be in a blue folder in the right-hand bottom drawer of the desk. If they're not there make a quick search of the other drawers. If you don't find them within ten minutes, come back here. If you do, don't let anyone else see them. Ask Escipión to send one of the maids with you. You mustn't go alone. Come and go by the back path. Don't switch on any lights. Use a torch only—there's one on the table over there." He saw the look of indecision on her face. "Don't worry about leaving me alone. I'm perfectly all right now," he smiled reassuringly, "and I can look after myself."

She had scarcely left when Basil returned, shaking his head. "There aren't any folders of any colour around. I've searched the passage and the linen cupboard, and asked Escipión if any had been handed to him. He gave me this handbook which he'd picked up himself."

The Inspector's shrug intimated that he was not surprised. "Did I hear someone go into Mr Warrack's room?" he asked.

"Yes, Gregory went in a minute ago. He'd been for a swim to get the stink of that cleaning fluid out of his system. He asked if there were anything he could do for you. When I said Miss Clegg was looking after you, he said he'd go along to the bar for a drink as soon as he'd showered and dressed. Where is Miss Clegg?"

158

"She's doing an errand for me. She'll be back very soon. I'd like you to go to the bar now, please, and, if they're not already there, get all the people from the bungalows to join you—Bill Eddow as well. Ask everyone to stay there until I come or send a message, and tell them that I'm none the worse for my—misadventure."

"I'll get them—and see that they stay." Basil watched the Inspector rise slowly and stand beside the bed. "Sure you're all right on your own?"

"Quite sure, thank you."

He heard Basil hurry down the passage and, going into the bathroom, filled the basin with cold water. When he came back into the bedroom he changed into clean clothes. Gingerly, as if he were handling a wren's fragile egg, he brushed his hair. The nausea seemed to have passed, if only temporarily, and he told himself that, apart from pain in head and neck, he had recovered sufficiently to face whatever was to come. Standing at the open window, Shadow nuzzling at his leg, he began to breathe in lightly, then more deeply. From somewhere near the Bar Felix came the sound of voices, then a hearty guffaw which he recognized as Perce's. His eye travelled past the renting bungalows which lay in darkness, past the bar and the dimly lit shop, and his headache was forgotten. Behind the louvred shutters of James's bungalow a light glowed which was too strong to have been produced by a torch. He looked at his watch. Miss Clegg had been gone for fifteen minutes. He was half way across the room when she came in, putting down her handbag with a thump on the table and laying the torch beside it.

"I think this is what you wanted," she said, but there was no uncertainty in the gesture with which she took some paper-clipped sheets from inside her blouse and handed them to him together with the bungalow key.

"Thank you. It is," he said after reading the first few lines of the top sheet. "Does whoever went with you know what this is?"

"No one else knows. I went alone."

"Alone." He looked at her with reproach. "Why didn't

you ask Escipión to send one of the maids with you?"

"He wasn't at the desk or in his office—and, as you'd told me to be quick, I went by myself." She opened her bag to disclose two substantial chunks of rock. "My cosh."

He smiled, thinking that she would have wielded her weapon effectively. "And now will you do something more for me?" He spoke quickly and urgently. "Will you try to find Mr Smurthwaite or Mr Arkell, preferably both of them." He detached the bottom sheet of the papers she had brought and, putting it into her hand, told her what she was to ask, adding, "If, as I hope, they can give you a definite opinion, I would appreciate a written certificate of identification. Then please go to the bar and ask Basil to bring the party he will have collected—and Carmen and Juan as well—to James's bungalow. I'd like them to arrive as soon as possible—you too, of course. And now I must go."

"You ought to be resting," she told him flatly.

"I'll be obedient as soon as it's all over," he promised, as he felt in his pocket to check that the screw of paper was still there. "Now you must obey me, please." He stooped to pat Shadow's head. "Stay here, Shadow," he said. Before Miss Clegg could speak he was out of the room. Crossing the hall, he met Escipión coming from the cloakroom and, cutting short the latter's worried inquiries, asked him to accompany Miss Clegg on her mission. "Don't let her out of your sight," he added as he hastened out.

The door of James's bungalow was closed, but splintered wood showed that it had been forced open by some sort of lever. It yielded to his push and he went in. Gregory was kneeling on the floor by the desk. Round him were scattered the contents of open drawers. He was stacking a pile of typed sheets as the Inspector entered. He looked up sharply, then gave a smile of relief. "Hullo. Glad to see you on your feet, and gladder still that you're here. I was starting to tidy up while I waited for somebody to come along. I didn't think the place should be left open and unguarded. As you see, someone's broken in. I think I saw him leaving—and he might return."

"Him?" The Inspector turned a chair and sat down.

"Well, someone in trousers. I was on my way to the bar when I saw him running round to the back. It was too dark to see anything more. My immediate thought before I saw that the place had been broken into was that it might be Juan, since Carmen has the key."

The Inspector shook his head. "I have the key in my pocket."

"Well, whoever it was obviously dispensed with a key— and, as I said, he was running as if he had to get away as quickly as he could. At any rate, I thought I'd better have a look—and this is what I found." Gregory put the stacked sheets into a drawer. "I expect it was one of those gipsies looking for cash."

"Perhaps." The Inspector bent to collect some sheets that had fallen to the floor when he sat down. Pain seemed to rip his head apart as he straightened up.

"You don't look too good." Gregory was concerned. "Can I get you anything—a glass of water, or there's bound to be some aspirins or something of the kind in the bathroom? Would you like to lie down for a short time?"

"No, I'll be all right in a moment, thank you."

"Sure?" Gregory picked up a batch of quarto sheets. "Part of a script." He put it aside. "The rest will be somewhere among this mess."

The Inspector looked at the sheets he had picked up. "Perhaps these." He read a few lines. "No, this seems to be a synopsis of some story. It looks as if you and Mr Rowley worked on it together. Aren't these notes in your handwriting?"

Gregory took the proffered sheets. "Looks like mine." He began to read. "Well, well, fancy this turning up. It's an idea for a script which I typed up ages ago. Then, when James and I were collaborating, I remembered it, looked at it again, added a few pencil notes about possible alternatives and gave it to him to read with the idea that we might work on it together. He was kind about it, but said he was too busy at the time. A month or two later he went off to the States and, as the idea seemed too promising to sit on indefinitely, I decided to write it up as a book in the hope that, if it were published, someone might make an offer for the film rights and, perhaps, ask me to work on the script." He laid the sheets on the desk and bent to pick up some of the scattered papers. "I wonder if the chap who made this mess pinched anything. We'd better have a look round the rest of the place."

"Yes, later." The Inspector spoke absently. He was listening to the sound of approaching voices.

Gregory cocked his head. "Somebody coming." Straightening a sheaf of papers by rapping them on the floor, he dropped them into a drawer and rose as Miss Clegg entered. She turned an anxious eye on the Inspector and, receiving a reassuring smile, nodded a vigorous affirmative towards two pieces of paper in her hand. Behind her came Antonia and Basil, Colin and Thersie, Carmen and Juan, Escipión, and, finally, Perce and Jack, the latter pushing Bill before him. They stared round the room in patent surprise.

"Quite a gathering," Gregory observed. "Anyone know anything about this?" He pointed at the paper-strewn floor and the open desk drawers.

"If anyone does, he's scarcely likely to say so unless he can convince us that he was preparing material for a paper-chase," Basil commented. "Isn't the first question 'Has anything been taken?'—and the second 'When did this happen?' "

"I can't answer the first. But, about ten minutes ago as I was on my way to the bar, I saw a light here and someone in trousers making a quick get-away. As the place was supposed to be locked up, I came along—and found this." Gregory made a comprehensive gesture. "The Inspector joined me a few minutes later as I was starting to put things straight." He looked round unsmiling. "I don't for a moment imagine it was any of us here, but if you care to say where you all were it might simplify matters."

"It might." The Inspector's tone lacked any expression. It

was clear that he was waiting for the others to speak, to say what they had to say without any prompting from him.

"I think we were all in the bar," Carmen volunteered, "except the Inspector and Greg, of course, and Miss Clegg and Escipión who came in a couple of minutes ago to bring us along here."

"'Cept me, too," said Jack, "when I had a call o' nature and went out there just after Colin." His forehead wrinkled. "I didn't see you there, Colin?"

"I was sitting down." Colin was unembarrassedly matter-of-fact. "I heard you—or someone—using the urinal."

"Seems to me," Perce broke in abruptly, "we're wasting our breath. We don't know how long ago whoever was in this place broke in." The eyes turned to him did not notice Miss Clegg's interrogatively raised eyebrows or the Inspector's infinitesmal shake of the head. "It don't take a lot of brain to see that the Inspector's got the lot of us here because he reckons it could be one of us that done in Clarice and the other two and tried to knock him off today. Carmen says that can of cleaning stuff could have been lifted from outside the shop any time after six. So there's a couple of questions we need answers to. Who could have swiped it, and where was all of us when the Inspector was clobbered? And when we've the answer to the second one you mightn't have to look much further for the first. The rest of you can speak for yourselves. Jack and me was coming round the side of the hotel and we didn't know nothing was happening till we heard Shadow raising the roof and someone crashing at the door of the cupboard. And we can speak for Gregory 'cos we saw him going into the hotel and starting to run."

"Antonia and I had come from the pine-wood," said Basil, "and were passing the back of the hotel when we heard Shadow barking and the Inspector trying to kick the door down. I climbed in at a passage window and managed to break the door open. Gregory arrived a few seconds later."

Gregory nodded agreement. "I heard the racket as I came up the steps. Escipión was in his office and jumped up to follow me."

"I was in my own room," Miss Clegg stated crisply.

"And I was with the kids and Juan out at the back tinkering with an engine. As far as I know, only Enrique was in the bar until I looked in just as Bill came along with Millie." Carmen turned in question to Bill. "That was about seven, wasn't it?"

"A few minutes after. We'd been for a walk up to Cap Tabal." As if he sensed doubt in someone's mind, Bill added truculently, "Millie will tell you the same."

"And where were you, Colin?" asked Gregory.

"With Thersie. We've been together all day on the beach or on the terrace of my—of my aunt's house."

Bill's eyes were on Thersie. After a momentary hesitation he said to her, "Didn't Millie and I see you going into your own bungalow as we were on our way to the bar?"

"Yes, it'll have been me," she agreed. "I went to put on some slacks while Colin was having a shower. I was only there for a very short time, and Colin was coming out of the bathroom when I got back."

"So none of us could have done it." Perce met his brother's glance. "Unless one or two of us isn't telling the truth."

"Or unless the apparent truth is deceptive." The Inspector had been listening with half-closed eyes. Now he opened them and moved his chair so that the light over the desk shone over his left shoulder. "I think we may be here some time," he continued, "so I suggest that we pick up the remaining papers from the floor and then sit down." He waited until everyone was seated, then began quietly, "A number of you gave me accounts of your actions last Monday which were untrue and which you were subsequently compelled to revise. I have not yet been able to check fully your amended accounts, and it may not be necessary to do so. I believe I know what is true and what is not, but I must be sure before I take any action. I said a few moments ago that the apparent truth can be deceptive. It could be, for instance, in Mr Warrack's case."

"What on earth do you mean?" Gregory was taken aback.

"If you're speaking of the attack on yourself, you know I couldn't have made it. I wasn't even in the hotel at the time. Damn it all, Perce and Jack saw me outside, and Escipión saw me as I ran through the hall."

"That was after I'd been attacked," the Inspector reminded him. "What were you doing beforehand?"

"Taking a breath of air on the beach, stretching my legs after sitting for most of the day."

"Did you speak to anyone, or was there anyone on the beach who might have seen you?"

Gregory frowned, then shook his head. "I don't remember seeing a soul—but I wasn't looking for anyone in particular."

"Then you can offer no unassailable alibi for the vital time. Just supposing, if I may, that it was you who attacked me—you could have gone into your room immediately afterwards, jumped the few feet from the balcony and reached the hotel steps as Perce and Jack came round the corner."

Gregory rubbed his cheek. "I suppose I could—though I didn't. Unless someone says he saw me, I obviously can't prove where I was." He thought for a moment. "But, if I haven't got an alibi, who has? Perce and Jack support each other's story. I'm not suggesting they haven't told the truth, but they can't prove it any more than I can. And doesn't the same thing apply to Antonia and Basil, and to Thersie and Colin? I mean, any of them could have pre-arranged an alibi story if they needed to do so, or agreed one afterwards. And isn't Escipión in the same boat as I am? He could have run back to his office in time for me to find him there as I dashed past."

Escipión shrugged his shoulders as if the suggestion were not worth any comment.

"You know, Greg's right enough there," said Jack. "We ain't none of us got alibis what would stand on their own two feet."

"Thanks, Jack." Gregory waited in case anyone appeared disposed to discuss the point further. "Let's go back to the cleaning fluid, shall we? Which of us could have taken it from wherever it was?"

"Anyone," said Perce. "Any of us could have nicked it from outside the shop when there was no one to see."

Bill, who had been listening glumly, suddenly sat forward. "Won't there be someone's prints on the can?"

"There'll be the Inspector's and Basil's and mine and probably a few others from people who handled it before and after," Gregory commented with mild impatience. "Let's try to get onto firmer ground. I take it we're all agreed that whoever attacked the Inspector did so because he or she thought he'd found some evidence that identified them with the deaths of James and the Pooles, and with which they could tamper while he was incapacitated. Is that right?" Accepting the Inspector's slight nod as comfirmation, he spread his hands in a gesture almost of apology. "Well, that seems to let me out, doesn't it?" he addressed the Inspector. "You and I know that I have an alibi for the time of the drownings."

The Inspector's head moved slightly. To Antonia it looked as if he found the effort to speak greater than he could make; but Gregory interpreted it differently. "An alibi," he repeated, "and a witness to it. Millie was with me in my room, as she's told you, from about noon to after four o'clock. You haven't any doubt that she told you the truth, have you?"

"None at all."

"Then that's that." His expression as he looked round the room was contrite. "I'm sorry. I meant to keep Millie's name out of this discussion, but I let it slip. I'd be grateful if you didn't let her know. She told the Inspector what she did solely to protect me from any suspicion. It was a damned generous thing to do, and I'd hate her to know that I've blown the gaff." He sighed as he took out a packet of cigarettes. "About time I piped down, I think, and let the Inspector quiz someone else."

"Before I do that there's a matter which we were discussing before the others arrived." The Inspector picked up the paper-clipped sheets from the desk. "This manuscript, which

166

was found in this room, is one which Mr Warrack tells me he typed up some years ago and asked James Rowley to read. It is the synopsis of a story which Mr Warrack hoped they might jointly turn into a film script. Mr Rowley apparently liked the story, but was too busy at the time to offer collaboration. Shortly afterwards he went to America. Mr Warrack then decided to turn the story into a book which, as some if not all of you know, has just been published. Somewhat surprisingly, another book which I have read in manuscript has without doubt been written from the same synopsis. It is, perhaps, fortunate that this other book has not been published, since Mr Warrack might well feel resentful at finding that his plot and ideas have been made use of by another writer."

"By another writer," Gregory repeated incredulously. "Who?"

"James Rowley. He had completed the manuscript when he died."

"James! I don't believe it. Good Lord, James was bubbling with invention. He never needed to pick anyone else's brains. It's not poss—"

"Surely," Basil's calm voice interrupted. "Surely writers often have the same or similar ideas?"

"The synopsis was among Mr Rowley's papers," the Inspector said levelly.

"Yes, we don't dispute that if you say so, but," Gregory's tone was earnest, "what I do dispute is that James would deliberately have used my or anyone else's ideas unless he thought he had a right to do so. I can't remember now what I said when I handed him the synopsis, but I may very well have given him the impression that, if we weren't going to work together on the script, I had no use for it. In any case, what does it matter now?" His forehead creased. "Perhaps I'm being stupid, but are you quite sure that the plot of James's book is the same as mine? I thought Carmen was the only one here who'd read *No End of a World*."

"Your book was lying on the bar counter, and I happened to read the résumé on the dust jacket. I can assure you that the main plot is the same in each case—and so is the name of the town where the action begins." The Inspector spoke

167

with certainty. "Finding this out must have given James Rowley a severe shock."

Gregory looked puzzled. "But James couldn't have read my book. It wasn't published until after he left England."

"He read the copy you lent Carmen."

"I let him have it 'cos he was a friend of yours, and he said you'd want him to read it," Carmen explained.

"Yes, of course I would," Gregory agreed. "Poor James," he went on regretfully. "The Inspector's right. It must have given him a hell of a shock to find he'd spent months writing a story which he couldn't send to any publisher or tell anyone about. I thought he seemed dispirited and oddly nervous when I broached the possibility of another collaboration last Sunday night. Coming on top of his long illness, this must have been a shattering blow. I wonder if— No," he shook his head, "James had too much self-respect."

Basil, who had been gazing thoughtfully at the ceiling, frowned. "Was James's manuscript in the folders you asked me to look for?" he asked the Inspector.

"It was." The Inspector had taken a screw of paper from his pocket and was beginning carefully to untwist it.

"But someone had already found and removed them."

"Presumably because their existence threatened that someone's safety." The Inspector flattened the twist of paper, disclosing two capsules, one red, the other pink and white. Turning in his chair, he pulled apart the red capsule and placed the empty half-cylinder on the desk. The other half, which was filled almost to the brim with a whitish powder, he propped against an ashtray. The onlookers watched in craning silence. He then took the white half from the second capsule, set aside the pink part and, picking up the red powder-filled half-capsule, slid the white half-cylinder onto it. Round him the others stared, question corrugating the intent faces. Perce breathed heavily, Brian frowned, a gasp of what might have been enlightenment came from Basil, Miss Clegg's expression tautened.

Putting down the newly assembled red-and-white capsule on the desk, the Inspector turned as if he were about to explain his actions. Casually he consulted his wrist watch. Finger and thumb moved as if he were adjusting the hands of the watch. "There is another point to be dealt with," he observed, as if he had decided that explanation would be superfluous. "I think that most of us cannot fail to know that Mr Arkell and his partner are experts in all kinds of office machinery. Yesterday Mr Arkell mentioned that he had offered to obtain an electric typewriter for you, Mr Warrack. You declined, saying that you had never used one." He pointed a finger at Miss Clegg. "Would you please read out what is written on the smaller sheet of paper in your hand?"

Heads turned in clockwork unison as she read in a clear, level voice, " 'We have no doubt that the typescript which we examined was typed on a Benson Electrotyper, Model No. 2.' The statement is dated today and signed by Oliver Smurthwaite and Harry Arkell."

"And to what typescript do they refer?"

"This." She held up a quarto sheet. "It is the final sheet of half a dozen which you asked me to bring you from this bungalow shortly after you had been attacked. The other five sheets are there," she pointed, "on the desk."

"Do you know the subject of the complete typescript?"

"I know what you told me."

"And what was that?"

"That it is the synopsis of the book which James Rowley was revising when he died. Which means that—" her pause was deliberate, the pause of a life-long teacher impressing a point on her audience, "—which means that it is also the synopsis of the novel written by Mr Warrack—who has never used an electric typewriter."

In the few seconds that ensued before the full import of the disclosure came to the others, Gregory acted. Glancing assessingly at the three men who were between him and the door, he pivoted and moved swiftly to the back of the room. By the time the others had risen he had snatched from the wall one of the pair of gleaming Toledo swords.

"So you pinched his story and killed him and the two poor bloody folk that saw you." Jack pushed his way forward, jaw set, bunching his fists.

Gregory whipped the blade menacingly. "Don't come any

169

nearer," he said sharply. "I'm a pretty useful swordsman."
As he spoke he stepped sideways towards the passage door
and felt behind him for the handle.

"Chuck something at him, Colin." Perce picked up a
chair by the back and pointed the legs at Gregory. "Get
another chair, Jack, and we'll pin him down."

The china ornament that Colin threw shattered against the
wall as Gregory dodged. The second missile, a heavy glass
ashtray, caught him off balance and smacked into his
upraised right wrist. As Perce and Jack moved forward, the
sword dropped hilt downwards from Gregory's hand and tee-
tered. Reaching down desperately, Gregory slipped on the
waxed tiles. His fingers had not touched the hilt when the
blade entered his body immediately below the rib-cage. A
high-pitched cry of surprise, a gasp, a convulsive twitch, and
he lay without movement.

Dropping the chair, Perce bent over the fallen man.
"Looks as if the bugger's killed hisself too," he remarked
dispassionately.

Palely determined, Thersie came forward with the Inspector, to kneel beside the body. It was apparent to both that no
first-aid treatment was needed, that the sword had pierced
Gregory's heart and that life was extinct.

In the cold shock that is the aftermath of violence and
horror the others waited until the Inspector rose to his feet.
Asking Escipión to take his car and summon the Civil
Guards and a doctor, he accompanied Colin and Jack as
they carried the dead man into the bedroom and laid him on
the bed of the man he had killed. During the few minutes
they were absent, Perce had taken practical measures.
Somewhere he had found a bottle and glasses. "A nip'll do
us all a world of good," he was saying as he splashed brandy
into a glass and, seeing the Inspector at his elbow, put it into
his hand.

The Inspector took a sip, and then another. His headache
had eased, but he felt drained of energy. With a murmur of
apology he sat down.

"Want one of us to stay?" asked Perce. "Or shall we take

ourselves off and wait in the bar in case you wants us later on?"

"I'd like you to stay for a few minutes so that I can explain and apologize for involving you all in this unpleasant situation. It would have been unwise for me to remain alone for long with someone who had little doubt that I knew him to be a murderer and who might well make a second attempt to save his own life at the expense of the man he feared could prove his guilt. But, infinitely more important," he smiled slightly, "I had no proof of his guilt. It was thus necessary to condition him into thinking not only that I suspected or knew everything but that I could also establish it. And that is why I wished you all to be here to listen to his answers. When a man has only one questioner and one listener his mind is directed to that single person. He can concentrate on that one man, ask himself what is behind a particular question and endeavour so to answer it that he does not commit himself irretrievably. And, if he makes a mistake, there is no witness. But he cannot so easily concentrate on a number of listeners. He does not know whether any of them may be in a position to query or to refute a statement. The more he is compelled to say, the greater his fears. The pressure on him increases until he can no longer stand it unless he is either innocent or a man of immensely strong character. If he is a hollow man like Gregory Warrack he loses his judgment and self-control and, in so doing, acknowledges his guilt."

"But you already knew that he had a motive, surely?" said Colin. "He had stolen the theme of James's book."

"I did not know that with certainty, even when it was proved that he could not, as he claimed, have typed the synopsis. He had only to say that he now remembered that one of the secretaries at the film studio had typed it for him —and it would have been difficult, if not impossible, after such a lapse of time, to have proved otherwise. On another point—a conversation which Thersie overheard—he could have said that he had confessed to James and that, James being a kindly man, they had come to some agreement on the matter, perhaps some financial arrangement. At the end of that conversation Thersie thought she heard James say something about letting the Lord decide, as if he were commenting about a matter on which a decision might depend on circumstances—health, for instance, or some question of chance. It was not until yesterday that it occurred to me that what James said could equally well have been 'We must let the law decide', thus warning Warrack that he would have to face a court action from which he would emerge financially ruined and with a reputation that would affect his whole future as a writer."

"And for him the only solution was murder," Miss Clegg said bleakly.

"That was what I thought, but it still had to be established. He had devised an alibi which would be confirmed by a completely honest witness. If I could show him how that alibi had been contrived, he would not, I hoped, realize that the demonstration was solely a product of deduction and impossible, without his confession, to prove."

"You're speaking of the capsules." Basil gestured towards the desk.

The Inspector nodded. "The red capsule contained a small dose of a hypnotic called Seconal; the pink and white capsule an anti-histamine called Benadryl. These were the means by which he planned that Millie should provide his alibi. Her personality defect—her eager sexuality—was obvious, and he decided to take advantage of it. He arranged with her to plead indisposition and cry off the tour to Ampurias so that they could spend the afternoon together in his room. I believe that on Sunday night he gave her more to drink than she was used to, so that she should feel unwell the next morning and willingly take the Benadryl capsule he sent her by Beryl. When she came to his room he reminded her that it was time to take a second dose; but the capsule he gave her was one of Seconal from which he had taken one of the red half-cylinders, replacing it by the white half of a Benadryl capsule. In a room with the blinds drawn it was unlikely that Millie, with her mind on other matters, would notice the small difference in the appearance of the capsule. She would probably swallow it without a glance—and very soon it would put her soundly to sleep for an hour or two. He knew, as did most of you, that James would be at La Caleta—and, almost certainly, the only person there. When Millie fell asleep he dropped from his balcony and went through the cleft. I think, though this is something we shall never know, that he found James floating on his back and jerked his head below the surface. The water rushed up James's nose, and at once he lost consciousness."

"Like the Brides in the Bath," Basil commented grimly.

"Exactly. At that moment the Pooles must have arrived in the bay just as their engine ran out of fuel. With one murder on his hands, Warrack did not hesitate to drown the witnesses. Then, returning to his room by the balcony, he dried himself and woke Millie."

"But, if she didn't wake till then, she couldn't give him no alibi for the time he wasn't there, could she?" The bristles on Perce's jaw rasped as his hand passed over them.

"But she did—and the explanation must again be conjectural. I believe that, before he woke her, he put back the hands of her wrist watch and of a travelling clock and placed the latter beside her, so that it would be she who checked and could later confirm the time."

"But how did he contrive to put them forward again so that Millie went back to her room before the Ampurias party returned and the Civil Guard came to ask for his help in finding the bodies?" asked Basil.

"He told her shortly after four o'clock, actual time, that she must leave soon and sent her into the bathroom for a shower. Naturally she—or possibly he—took off her wrist watch and, while she was out of the room, he altered the hands of both timepieces to match the time on his own watch."

"And nobody saw him creeping in or out by the balcony," Jack observed soberly. "The Devil was looking after his own all right."

"He chose a time when everyone would be serving or eat-

173

ing lunch. He had been told what the other visitors would be doing. If he had seen anyone he would have waited for another time and made another plan." The Inspector raised his head. Into the stillness came the sound of approaching cars. "I think it would be best if you would leave me to deal with my colleagues," he said. "If they should wish to see you, I will let you know." He went towards the window, then turned. "Please don't say anything to anyone tonight about what has happened—above all, nothing to Millie. I will tell her myself."

Miss Clegg waited for the others to leave before she said, "I was going to volunteer to tell Millie that Gregory was dead, but I'm thankful not to have to do so. I shouldn't be able to tell her without letting my own feelings about him become evident."

"You had your own suspicions about him, didn't you?" he asked.

"Suspicion based on little but instinct. There's little that the complete egoist will not do. And, as I think I said to you yesterday, he lacked imagination. All his thinking was basically second-hand. A more imaginative man would have realized that he could convince the not very intelligent Pooles that he had tried and failed to save James from drowning, and he would have had them to testify to the efforts he had made. He could have awakened Millie to tell her that, while she was asleep, he had heard James calling out and had rushed to his aid. Why should anyone have doubted that a sick man's death was accidental?" She stopped abruptly. "I'm talking too much. You look all in."

He smiled. "I haven't felt better for a long time."

In the Bar Felix they were talking soberly about what had just happened. Bill made little contribution to the conversation. When directly addressed he replied absent-mindedly. His thoughts were about his own predicament, about the penalty that might be exacted for the smuggling which he had so light-heartedly undertaken. Escipión was wondering how much any mention of the Hotel Adrián in the press reports would affect bookings for the next season. Cynically he came to the conclusion that it might bring more clients, eager to visit the scene of the tragedies, to extract morbid pleasure from photographing the places and some of the people involved. From time to time someone looked out of the windows at the cars standing outside the bungalow. It was with a feeling of relief that they heard the metallic slam of doors and the whirr of starter motors.

"Think one of us should pop along and see if the Inspector's O.K.?" asked Perce.

Miss Clegg shook her head. "No, I'm sure he'd rather be left alone for the time being. If he wants to talk to anyone he'll come along here."

Colin put his hand on Thersie's wrist. "Would you like to come for a walk?" he suggested softly.

Thersie nodded, and with understanding smiles the others watched them go. They walked down the beach and turned towards Cap Tabal. It was some time before either of them spoke.

"I've been thinking," Colin began, then stopped.

After a moment she gave an encouraging "Uhm?"

"Your parents will be here tomorrow, won't they?"

It was a question to which he knew the answer; but since she realized that he needed a response she said "Yes."

"Will you be going back to England with them?"

"Yes, to London. I haven't seen much of them lately. I think I might look for a job and stay with them, at any rate for the winter."

"I'll have to leave early next week, Thersie. I must go and see my aunt's housekeeper and talk to a lawyer and try to get things settled as far as possible. Then I shall have to get back to Manchester. But I could come up to London at week-ends—if you'd like me to."

"I'd like it," she said simply.

"A friend of mine in Hampstead would put me up. He has a flat in Tanza Road."

"In Tanza Road." She smiled. "But that's only ten minutes walk from where we live."

He didn't tell her that he already knew, that he had asked Carmen for her parents' address. Abruptly he straightened, gazing into the distance. "I'm in love with you, Thersie," he said, almost curtly, then turned to face her.

"And I like you very much." She took his hand. "But we've only known each other for four days."

"Four and a half." It was a simple statement of fact, not a correction. He gazed into the candid eyes that were nearly level with his. "Isn't that long enough for falling in love?"

"Yes," she said. "It's long enough." She was thinking of the man to whom she had once been engaged. "But it's not long enough for one to know whether one's going to stay in love."

"And how long would that take, Thersie?"

"I don't know. I don't know, Colin." She raised his hand to her cheek, and suddenly she was smiling. "But we could find out."

The Inspector was once more alone in the bungalow. He heard the car doors slam and, standing in the doorway, watched the vehicles jolt slowly to the main road. The night was now clear, the star-studded sky a scintillant backcloth to the sea that lapped peacefully towards a never-reached goal. From the Bar Felix came a murmur of voices and the occasional clink of a glass. Across the beach, lamps shone on the terrace and in the hall of the Hotel Adrián, and there was light from one of the bedroom windows. From the west an offshore breeze carried the insistent call of love-seeking crickets.

He sat down on the doorstep and took out his cigarette case. Two hours ago it had seemed to him that he had reached the limits of endurance. His head had been racked by surges of excruciating pain, his legs seemingly without bone or muscle. Now there was only a background ache. Lighting a cigarette, he considered his actions of the past few days and, as always at the end of a murder investigation, began to censure himself that he had allowed the quarry to elude him for so long. He should have realized from Millie's confession that she had gone to sleep during her afternoon of love. Gregory's appearance, at a moment when James's bungalow was unlocked, and his offer to send off James's manuscript were in retrospect some of the pointers to which he had been blind. Others were that Gregory had, according to Millie, relied on her checking the time until he had taken charge of the clock and returned it to where one would have expected to find it—on the bedside table; that the capsules which Beryl gave to Millie had been provided by Gregory. Small points, but what was now part of a clear pattern. The Seconal bottle which had been among Basil and Antonia's rubbish must have been put in their bucket by Gregory when he stopped by it that morning ostensibly to light a cigarette. Empty or not, it was something he would be wise to get rid of. Whether it carried his fingerprints was now a matter of academic interest only.

That so many of the possible suspects had lied to him was to be expected; for there are few people who have nothing to conceal. There had been good reason to disbelieve the story that Perce and Jack had told. In his mind there was little doubt that they had raised the gold from the sunken launch and smuggled it into England; little doubt, but no proof. Nor would proof, he thought, ever be found. They were, as he had overheard Perce saying, a couple of fly blokes. Thirsty flies, too. He smiled.

Basil, he felt sure, had been the man behind the bank robberies—and the man who had made the tape that had brought to birth the Conscience Fund. An idealist, a man of bold action—and a criminal. But a man with the strength of his opinions, a man whom one was glad to have known.

And Miss Clegg . . .

Her name reminded him that he still had a task to perform. He was wondering where he might find Millie when a pair of strolling figures rounded the banjo before the Pooles' house. Arms round each other's shoulders, heads touching, they approached, oblivious of all except themselves. They started when he spoke, and Cyril's arm dropped self-consciously to his side.

"She was with us till we said we were off for a walk," Beryl replied to his question, "and then she said she'd be off to bed. What's been going on here? Cars and cops, and everyone in the bar saying it'd keep till morning as if they were talking about a jug of milk."

The Inspector smiled. "Perhaps they were."

"Oh, get on with you," she exclaimed scornfully. "If you're not going to tell us, Cyril and me's got something better to do than to stand here, haven't we, me lad?" She tucked his arm round her as he made some inaudible mutter, and led him away.

Millie half raised her head as she heard the knock on the door. "Come in," she called, wondering why Beryl had not arrived as she usually did with a rattle of the handle and a shove at the door that sent it thudding against the wall. When she saw the Inspector she hastily pulled the sheet up to her chin, astonished beyond speech.

"Can I talk to you, Millie?" he asked. The deep voice was friendly, but to Millie he seemed a little unsure of himself. A thought entered her mind, but she dismissed it as being unlikely. He must know that Beryl might come in at any minute.

"If you want to," she said uncertainly.

He looked round the room and, seeing the two chairs heaped with discarded clothes, perched himself on the end of the bed. She lay, hugging the sheet, watching him through wide-open eyes, her blond hair ruffled, a slight sheen of perspiration on her forehead, pretty and innocent.

"If you'd like to sit up," he suggested, "I'll find your dressing-gown."

"I can't." She gave a little grin. "It's so hot I'm sleeping raw."

"I wanted to talk to you while you were by yourself," he said gently, "to tell you that Gregory is dead."

"Dead," she repeated; then, as understanding hit her, "Dead!" Her voice became a whisper. "But he can't be."

"It was a kind of accident, Millie, but perhaps for him a

178

merciful one. If he had lived he would have had to stand trial for murder."

"For murder?" she uttered in a strangled croak.

"He killed James Rowley and Mr and Mrs Poole."

She stared at him, her eyes wide in incredulity. "But he couldn't have. He was with me."

Tomorrow, he was thinking, she will hear this from others. Someone will talk. It is better she should know now. "He gave you a sleeping pill and, while you were asleep, he went out. He made the plan on Sunday, to use you to confirm his alibi. You mustn't regret his death, Millie. He was ruthless and inhuman and incapable of affection."

"But I liked him," she said in a small voice as if to herself. She lay still, her eyelids screwed up tightly. Soon her face began to pucker and tears came. Suddenly she screamed. "I let a murderer make love to me—a *murderer*." The next moment she had thrown back the sheet and was clinging to him, her head buried in his neck, her body shaking as she sobbed. He held her to him, one hand on the fair head, the other on the soft skin of her back. Comfort was all he could offer, kindness, a reassurance that her world had not been shattered. What more could he do than continue to hold her? In a little time her sobs began to ease and he felt her grip tighten. The tear-wet face pressed into his neck. The next moment he felt her lips move and, with a quickening of the heart, realized that she was blindly seeking the release that was natural to her. Her firm young breasts pushed against his shirt and her hand moved downwards. Then he heard the door open.

A pair of sun-tanned hands took Millie by the wrists and held them so that he was able to disengage himself. He stood up to meet the sympathetic, concerned and, it seemed to him amused, eyes of Miss Clegg.

"I thought you might need a friend," she whispered. "Off you go now. It's my turn to relieve you of your Candy."

Envoi

THE INSPECTOR SAT, shirt-sleeved, in his office in Barcelona. Through the slats of the Venetian blind December sunshine barred the black-tiled floor with gold. He was at the moment alone at his desk, but his thoughts were far away from the papers that lay before him. He was looking at the framed picture in his hand. It was an enlargement from a colour negative that he had taken the previous week on the balcony of his flat. Benita had not known that he was there until she heard the click of the camera shutter. She was sitting, her head bent, her eyes on the baby on her lap. Happiness and fulfillment lit the pro-filed face. Shadow stood, forepaws on the arm of the chair, peering curiously at the infant, her wagging tail a blur of movement.

He put down the frame as a messenger knocked at the door and, entering, placed on the desk two envelopes and a small, sealed, registered parcel. English stamps, he noted, as he slit one of the envelopes and extracted a letter and a snapshot.

Dear Friend,
    Thought you might like to see what the missuses and the kids look like. We come unexpected-like into a bit of money, and what's at the back of us is the foundations of a little factory we're setting up for ourselfs. If things goes

180

O.K. we'll all be out next year. Send us your phone number and we'll give you a tinkle.

Hoping to see you.

Perce and Jack.

In the snapshot the two men grinned widely as if at a shared joke. On Perce's right a handsome, buxom woman holding a plump baby waved at the camera. On Jack's left an equally comely and well-fleshed wife appeared to be stifling laughter. At either end of the group stood a sturdy boy of about six. How much they resembled their parents it was impossible to say, for each had his tongue stuck out to its fullest extent.

Smiling, the Inspector opened the second envelope. Basil had written:

Dear Inspector,

I think you will be glad to know—though I'm sure you already knew—that Antonia and I have again gone into partnership, this time for life. An event expected in July will probably prevent us from coming to Spain next year, but we hope to be in Cala Felix the following one and, in happier circumstances, to renew our friendship.

Antonia was rummaging in a drawer the other day and found something which we thought we'd like to send you. Perhaps you would accept it as a sort of 'thank-you' for not pursuing, as I think you could well have done, certain breaches of the law. I'm posting it separately in the hope that it may keep us in your memory until our next meeting.

Breaking the sealed ends of the packet, the Inspector opened the box and removed a wad of tissue paper. On a pad of cotton wool lay a gold signet ring set with a lapis lazuli. Taking it to the window, he held it beneath one of the louvres of the blind. A tilt away from the light, and he was able to read the intertwined letters incised in the stone. S.B. —his own initials. Reversed they were Basil's. Thoughtfully he eased it over the second joint of his little finger.

He was again smiling as he returned to his chair and looked again at the two letters and the snapshot. There was something disarmingly youthful, ingenuous, endearing—and a little smug—about the English sense of humour.